Broken

Broken

Carmen N. Arenas

Romance

BROKEN

Printed in US July 2025
ISBN: 979-8-9889305-9-4 Paperback
Edited by Irma Ruiz
Published by Sula Too Publishing, Tampa, Florida
Printed in the United States.

"The old have memories, the young have visions."
                     - An Old African Proverb

"Youth is wasted on the ugly." – Me - C N Arenas

"Under pressure she became a diamond, under pressure she became unbreakable." - R.H. Sin

"Some people lose diamonds in search of stones." -
                           - Unknown

"And Still I Rise"- Maya Angelou

CHAPTER 1

Let's just say that I have always been a bit challenged in my decisions, especially lately when it comes to Alexander Sterling. I do have a big heart and at times it consumes itself with lost causes. At least that is what I believe is my saving grace. Now that I am about to turn the big 4-0 (gulp) I realize that I need to reevaluate some things in my life.

Let's go back two years. Why, you ask? That is when I made a huge decision and it created my reality, of where I am today. When I decided to give up my celibacy commitment agreement, I thought, "hell" and that is when I began screwing around with my ex-husband. It started with me just trying to take the 'edge' of". My life's issues were mounting up, and I missed having sex as a regular part of my life. I know that is a lame excuse, but I was under a lot of stress. Really! Seriously!

Our story is a long, complicated one, and any sane person would not believe what we have put each other through. Correction: What he has put me through and why on earth would I take him back?!?!? I was lonely. Being with him was comfortable. Whatever the reason(s), I started a physical relationship with Alexander again.

We managed to be on friendly terms for our three beautiful children; and since we were together for such a huge part of our lives, it was difficult to not be in each other's lives. Our families have always been close. We grew up together. Plus, maturity had to win out; and our three children (Avery, Aren, and Alexis) did not have to lose everything when we divorced. When Alexander's second wife left him, he turned to me for support.

Sure, good ol' Mercedes to the rescue. The stand-up gal that I am, I was available to be his "comfort". Hell, who better than I, knows how to get over a lousy ex? I have been going through it for 7 years now. Never mind the fact that the relationship he is now ending is the one that left us broken.

Alexander and I did not just jump into bed together as soon as Raemier left, but it was not too long after. It began somewhat slowly. He would call to vent how nasty of a person she is. How she set him up, so she could move out. How Raemier messed up his life. How horrible she is, how she did this and that. I loved hearing the hardships she had caused him, because I enjoyed that he suffered a little or as much as I had from their betrayal. Then his calls were repentant of his choices, the choices he made that upturned our lives. How he "missed what we had." He missed our family and the life we were building and had built. He was a fool, etc.…

The kind of conversations I entertained because I had always wanted to hear them from him since the day he left us. The kind of conversations that vindicated me and the unspoken "I told you so's" resounding in my head.

Then those few self-defeating calls of his, lamenting that he is a better demolition man (relationship-wise) than his day job as an investment banker/wealth manager/VC, considering what he put us through. (Ya-da, ya-da, ya-da!) Whatever! He needs to remain the brilliant hedge-fund, investment banker, wealth manager and venture capitalist that he is! Especially now that he will be taking care of three households, mine, his, and hers. Of course, with my household being the most important of all.

At least he was smart and had a prenuptial agreement with Raemier, so it should not be too bad with this divorce, if they do go through with it, that is.

When we married, we did not have a prenuptial and at the time of our divorce he was so laden with guilt that I got everything I asked for and then some. Since the divorce, I have been raising our children, and I just recently returned to school to complete my degree which I put on hold when we had our first son, Avery.

At 22 years old, I was "young & dumb" and on top of that I was (excuse my language) "dick-whipped" by Alexander. I can admit it. Grown women admit their flaws and while learning lessons, it shows growth. I was (again, excuse my language) DICK-WHIPPED and I loved every minute of it. That was a problem. We had known each other for years, because our grandmothers worked together for years.

I saw his philandering ways early on. We did not attend the same high schools, but we had a lot of the same friends. He often brought a different girl to every party we attended, even when he supposedly had a girlfriend. He was known to say, "Where one won't, another will." He was two years older than me, but I knew that he wanted to date me. We flirted incessantly. Of course, with him being two years older, my dad was not having that! So, nothing ever happened.

I arrived on his college campus two years after he went away to school and that became a different story. We were inseparable, but we still did not get together right away. He kept claiming that he wasn't ready for "us." He was still serial dating and being a rogue with a lot of hearts. I had no idea that a quarter of the female population on our campus (student and faculty alike) were well aware of and acquainted with his talents, and that he had the nickname "the talented Mr. Whipply." I was too green and naïve to the very obvious signs and warning lights flashing before my eyes. He began "dating" Shenay, a friend of mine, and that is when I should have given up on him -but I didn't. I casually dated a few guys. I even tried to make him jealous by dating a friend of his, but I was always waiting for Alexander to "pick me." Like I said, I was young and dumb. Shenay was falling hard for him, and I was growing more jealous by the minute. I warned her that he was trouble. She never knew of my feelings for Alexander. She just thought we were close - like a brother and sister. One summer when we both were back in Tampa, Alexander, myself and a few of our friends went out to celebrate my twenty-first birthday. Shenay drove to Tampa from Miami for the celebration. The group bar hopped in Ybor City, and we all ended up at Alexander's parent's house as the party continued. There we played various drinking games, card games, and music blared in his parent's pool house and outside on their lanai. Alexander grabbed me and we started to dance. Slowly we danced on his parent's lanai and the music was a lively song from 2Live Crew.

He looked in my eyes and whispered, that he had been watching me all night, and that he was finally ready for "us." What?!?!? I was drunk, but I was sobering up really fast. What is he saying? What about Shenay? As soon as I thought of her, she walks outside where we were. She sees us, and she isn't dumb. She knows his moves just as I do. He looks at her and smiles his $50-million smile. She looks at the two of us, she is devastated, and she turns and leaves. I try to go after her, and he stops me, holding onto my hand tightly. He turns me to him.

"Let her go. She knows already." He says.

"She knows what, exactly?" I ask.

"That I want to be with you. I told her before we left Tallahassee."

"You told her last month that you wanted to be with me?"

"Yes. She did not tell you?" He smiles again.

"No." No, she did not. I melt. I let him pull me closer. He tells me how he has finally decided that he is "ready" and that he had to be sure because he cannot mess up with me. I am his "forever lady." He is saying everything that I wanted to hear, but I know that I have just lost and hurt a good friend. You would have thought that I would have still run after my friend, making sure that she was alright. But I did not.

Young, dumb, and mean - yes, add mean. I just wanted Alexander. Finally!

It wasn't until several years later, I realized that there

was no victory the night of my twenty-first birthday, and I had won no prize in the young Alexander Sterling. I let Shenay leave and go back to Miami that night, and we never spoke again.

We dated while at home. I made him wait to have sex for those last 3 months of our summer.

When I drove up to his parents' house a night before we headed back to Tallahassee. One day, he took my breath away when he told me that he was a "very lucky man" No. I felt that it was I who was the lucky one. It was finally my turn, he chose me. He made me feel like I was the only one for him. I would learn many years later (in marriage counseling) that he and Shenay (and others) had sex a few more times, while I called myself "making him wait" and in between, also while we were in our several rough patches.

When we returned to Tallahassee that fall semester of my sophomore year, I finally slept with Alexander. We decided to move in together. Much to my parents' angst, but I was in love..

Our time dating was, for me, all I ever wanted. He courted me. He wooed me. When he looked at me, I knew that I was desired. I thought that I was loved by him. It turns out it was just lust.

For some reason, I thought that he would change his ways for me. Maya Angelou once told Oprah, "When someone shows you who they really are, believe them." I did not believe him. He always showed me that he could not be trusted with a girl or a woman's heart. I always imagined that he would not treat me like he treated the others, because he made me feel that I was different and that I was special. In the end, I felt as if I was just another girl, though he played me differently but ultimately the same.

I thought that the three-month rule was being followed by all parties involved. Our first time was magical to me. My 21-year-old self was not ready for what the young Alexander's talents would bring to my life. My mind became addled; and whatever problems we had, it was always settled in our boudoir. Something magical in that rhythmic friction. Soon, I was pregnant with Avery, and Alexander was finishing his 2 degrees, in Business Economics and Finance.

He and I began to have problems. He wanted to take a job in Orlando, and I wanted to stay and finish school. He said that I could go to school anywhere. Our family's opportunity was in Orlando. That was just the beginning of me putting my life on hold for him. It wasn't long before I realized that there was no one standing up for me, not even me.

How we began to rediscover each other in the bedroom that day, two years ago, came as a total need to de-stress. We were using each other to satisfy a need. No strings. No big deal, right? Wrong! I had no delusions of us getting back together. We were wrong for each other on so many levels, I know this! But after over 7 years of dating and then not dating as a celibate divorcee, yes celibate. I realized early on that sex muddles things up and I decided to abstain this time around. Well, that dried up a lot of my social calendar. Men aren't interested in middle-aged women who aren't giving up their goodies. Well sorry date number 1,137. My goodies are sacred, and I am saving them for Mr. Right, not Mr. Right now. Deal with it!

My physical frustration and stress began to escalate. Problems began to build up, and the children became pre-teens and teenagers. I developed stress headaches and knotted shoulders: Tension. Yes, that is my story, and I am sticking to it. You know of course that just would not do.

Then on top of everything I found "the letter." The

letter was from my grandmother to my grandfather. They were married for 70 years had six beautiful Afro-Cuban children, one being my dad. Although, I knew they were human, I always felt that they had an awesome, enduring love. That is until I found her letter to him. The pain I read in her words tore my heart apart. She described in heart aching detail how she felt when she saw my Abuelo's face light up when   his 91-year-old ass sees his obvious mistress while they were out together. Then, she described how throughout their marriage, she always knew about "the other women." But, to see his face light up was too much for her to bear.

She then asked him, in the letter, to leave her. He never left her, but she died six months later in bed sleeping next to him. Her doctors said the cause of death was an enlarged heart. I now think, it was from a broken heart. We will never know.

My Abuelo died one year and six months after she did. I thought his death was because he realized, life was nothing without her. Her death took place 16 years ago; but, now after reading this letter she wrote, it made me feel like I was losing them again. Now, I am pissed at my deceased Abuelo for breaking her heart. I now had a freshly opened wound in my heart. The letter also created desperation in me to find a good relationship, quickly, because life is too short. And being single is not working for me, not that marriage did either.

As I held the letter in my hands, my phone rings. It is Alex informing me that Avery had not yet picked up his brother and sister from him and he is asking me to come over to get them; and so additionally, we can have a talk. My drive over to Alexander's was a blur. I am still very numb from my grandmother's letter.

When I arrive, not only has our 16-year-old already picked up his siblings but has already left for home.

Alexander had a delicious smelling meal prepared and the game of Trivial Pursuit is open ready for us to play. Alexander was talking and all I could see was my Abuelo's smiling face talking back at me. It is the face of the deceiver. Treachery was afoot but I have fastened on my blinders, and I walk into his home and close the door.

We play the game we play so well. No, not just the game of Trivial Pursuit but the game of "us." We talk politics. The wine is flowing. The salmon is superb. The conversation is great. Alexander was always a great, stimulating date. The game of Trivial Pursuit was intense, for we are both competitive. We discussed tech issues, my stock and mutual fund portfolios which he manages for me.

Then he leans over and grabs my leg. Oh! That damn, button pusher! He knows my inner thigh is my button number one.

"What are you doing?" I ask.

He smiles. "Nothing, I am just touching you."

"I can see and feel that." I said.

He touches my cheek. "You have a little sauce on your face. I am wiping it off. That is all."

"Yeah right."

He smiles again. That 40-year-old smile still looks like the 19-year-old. Wait, did I just melt? I think I did just feel myself melt a little! Wait! Am I smiling back? My body is betraying me! Just like all those years ago, what the hell is happening to me? And now he is kissing me?! And I am kissing him back?! Wait! No, wait!

"Wait" I'm finally able to say aloud after catching my breath.

"Why?" He asked me breathlessly.

"Just wait." I am trying to collect myself. "Why are you trying to seduce me?"

"So, you don't want me to?"

"No. That part of our lives is over."

"Speak for yourself!"

"No, I mean that part where we "do" each other is over."

"It was just a kiss, Mercey."

I love when he says my name. "And since when are our kisses 'just a kiss'?"

"Never are they 'just a kiss', but if that's all I can get, I will take it. I had to kiss you. I miss you. I never stopped missing you."

"Then what have the last seven years been? Oh, I know, you married to the other woman."

"We have only been married for three years and that is not the issue now. She is gone."

"But you are still married. And I will never be 'the

other woman'!"

"I may be married on paper only. But look around you. She is gone. She cleared out my entire house! Look for yourself."

He then pulled me by the hand to show me his partially furnished modern McMansion. I did notice the sparseness. But I would not ever point it out. I have simply too much class! I chuckle at his wounded look as he explains how she took his plasma televisions and left him to take out his old projectors from his storage so that he can watch television. Plus, how hard it is for him to cook without his special cookware. He then says "she's no you." What the hell does he mean by that? "She's no me?!" Of course not! She never would be! She was a downgrade from me - in my modest opinion. There is absolutely no comparison. He downgraded by at least 100 levels in my book. Snobbish of me, maybe, yes, but you do not know half the hurt and embarrassment they have put me through. But hey, I am no judge for his tastes! I just smirk at his poor attempt at a compliment and I follow him through the house as he continues to tour me about his home.

When he left us, he left everything behind and dumb me, I delivered his requested items to him. I did everything but hire a moving truck for him and literally placed everything on a platter. Whenever our kids came to his house for their overnight visits he would request more of his things. What was once "our house", became my and the kid's house.

The kids and I have a large newer house in a neighborhood surrounded by larger older homes. Alexander and I built the monstrous Italianate Mediterranean-styled stucco-covered design after the homes we saw in our travels to Italy and Spain, on trips we managed to take together throughout the early years of our marriage. We wanted our home to look like the old world and for us to have the look and appearance of the "old money" families that surrounded us. We paid enough to fit in, purchasing 3 lots in the most desirable part of South Tampa.

The home I am standing in now, is all modern and state-of-the-art, straight lines, 90 degree angles, and very sterile. I made him a home and he left it for this modern stark museum. His choice.

"Mercey?"

"Hmmmm, what?"

"I asked if you wanted another glass of wine."

"Sure."

"What has you so preoccupied?"

"I was just thinking. I have a lot on my mind."

"Like what? I am just talking away, and you are not even listening to me. You have always listened to my problems it is the least that I can do is to be a listening ear for you too."

"Well, it is nothing. I just... nothing. I am just tired and a little stressed."

"I have something for that stress."

I smirk again, "I remember well your talents for de-stressing. But no, No thank you."

He chuckles, "Why not? It would be good, I promise."

"Oh, because I have already told you why. You are married and I am celibate. Sex is messy and confusing with a relationship that is undefined. Again, no thank you." I move his hand off my arm, to emphasize my point.

"Why do we need definitions? Why can't we just be whatever we are? Divorced friends with the benefit of sexual satisfaction?"

"I think you are confused. Let me be clear, that is not who I want to be to you or anyone. Just because we are divorced and we are friendly, I do not think we should cross that line just because we're compatible with each other and have managed well at being just friends."

"Not that I want to change the subject. Do you know that was one of her main problems?"

"Whose?"

"Raemier. She could not figure out how you were still my friend after everything we put you through. She said that we still had to be getting it on."

I laugh. "You did correct her, didn't you? You did tell her that we had to be mature for the kids' sakes? Especially, when Avery and Aren both began acting out, we had to get over ourselves to be better parents. Surely, she could see that was all it was, right? Wait a minute, were you cheating on her?"

"No, when she and I got married I really was faithful to her."

Oww! Pain, his words were a sucker punch straight to my gut! I think I even winced when he said that because he reacted.

"Sorry." He says.

He's sorry. I start to walk away, but he grabs my hand. I try to pull away.

"Now her walls go up. You know that is what happened to us. You are so hard and you close off your heart too quickly. You shut me out."

"Excuse me? What? You are blaming me for the demise of our relationship?"

"No, I'm not blaming you. I just need you to know how it was for me. I needed someone, I needed you and you weren't there. Raemier always needed me."

"What and now she doesn't?"

"I left you because she needed me, and I knew that you would always be okay with or without me. You are always so strong. Like now, you are so heated. I can feel the fire jumping out of your skin. It excites me to see that you still feel something for me. My baby, mi Amore! I have come to the place in life, where I want the love and not the dependency of desperation Raemier offered me, she could never trust me enough to love me, as you did."

"Whatever! Let me let you know a little of what is bothering me. I just found a letter from my Abuelita to my Abuelo. It was in our family's old Bible. I was just going through it and … Well there it was tucked away in that old Bible for all these years. She described how she felt when she saw my Abuelo's face light up when his 91-year-old ass "bumped" into who was his obvious mistress. I know that feeling because of you! Wow, some of the women in my family must be cursed or something when it comes to the men we love. I always romanticized my "Abuelo's death as though he died because he could not live without my Abuela and he just stopped living because he loved her so much. But, now, I realize that maybe it was just the guilt he should have felt for not being the man she deserved. Maybe, it was that she took such good care of him and he did not know how to live on his own".

"All I do know, now, is that she died miserable and sad and she felt alone even with him sleeping right beside her for seventy years. Now, you tell me that I shut you out? That you aren't 'blaming me'. Be real, you are blaming me! You left me! You left our kids for another woman and your other kids! It ended as if I said 'it was okay'. I was your door mat. Back then, I may have felt I had no worth. But now, that time has passed, I know my worth. Asshole know this, I am priceless! And I deserved better than you. How you treated me was awful. I never felt good enough, that I was enough for you!"

"You are misunderstanding me. I am not just saying that… Fuck it. Just never mind."

He sounded irritated with me, but there he goes again with that smile of his creeping up slowly across his face. I just want to punch him in the mouth. He is so smug. Then in one quick move, he grabbed me by the waist and pulled me into his embrace.

"I am sorry about Señora Ynez. I knew them both and when I saw them, I saw them the same way you remember them. I do not doubt that they were in love with each other. Since we were kids, I only knew them as having the perfect marriage. It is what I wanted for us. Those days at the ballpark Mr. and Mrs. Quintero were who we looked up to. Believe that, Mercedes."

"You don't know. You didn't see her letter."

"You know we sometimes say things we don't mean when we are hurt. She could have left him, but she didn't." I let him pull me closer.

"And, she was hurt. He hurt her."

"And I have hurt you in our past, you forgave me. She must have forgiven him, so trust that. She knew who she was. You knew who she was."

I looked up at him, "oh I forgave you, did I? Don't be so sure of that!"

He kisses me, again. I let him.

His kisses are like tall glasses of cold water for my parched soul in my dry loveless desert. We linger in the kiss, exploring our familiar mouths. We fall into our old rhythms. I pull away from his hungry kiss, it is too late to play hard to get now! His mouth trying to claim me again as his, I allow myself to remain in his embrace. I place my head on his chest. I fall into what was once my spot, my groove, MY place. Oh, how I wish I still belonged there! Memories flood my mind of our first dance, our wedding reception, the births of our children, every scene where he held me like this.

"We fit so well together." Alex breaks the silence with his uncanny knack for speaking what I am thinking.

"Do not say that. I really do not need this, right now. I am too emotional and needy. I just may believe you."

"Why shouldn't you believe me?"

"Because, you have lied to me too many times."

"When? Lying is not my thing."

"The day before you left me and said that you loved me. Then you were gone - here to her."

"Mercey, damn it, stop do not do that. I never stopped loving you. You stopped loving me, and I left you for you to find your own happiness since I messed everything up for us. It was obvious that you were not happy with me."

"Don't you dare!"

He kisses me again, and I bite his bottom lip. "Don't you dare tell me you did not know that I loved you. I have forgiven you time and time again. I gave you my all!"

"Well, I could not see how you could love me after you found out that she was pregnant with twins. I felt you were just going through the motions when you did not leave me after that."

I winced again. I sigh. I am so heavy by all the raw emotions being exposed within me. I try to pull out of his embrace, but he holds me even tighter. His eyes plead with me telling me that he is earnest.

He says, "I am sorry."

I just look at him. His brown eyes are tearing. I want to look away from him, before the hurt shows. Too late. Memories again begin to replay in my head.

Raemier's words "Project Triplets". That rings in my ears to this very day. I remember her crashing my baby shower, her belly extended, much larger than my own. She was also carrying my husband's seeds. They were growing as my Aren grew within me. The looks on my family's faces, horrified but knowing, as that bitch taunted me. All eyes were on me. I was mortified. That did not stop her from showing up time and time again, karate tournaments for Avery, family barbecues, and beach outings. There she was, trying to make sure that I knew who she was and that she was in my life to stay if I chose to remain with Alex or not. I was angry. I was furious with Alex. Especially with how he handled her. He behaved as a coward, ashamed of his actions, ineffective in handling his stupid bitch-assed troll whore. Making me always look like a fool. And on top of everything else, she and I go into labor only hours apart from each other, in the same hospital. Seeing my husband torn for the first time, briefly confused, as to what he should do, he stayed with me, but I could tell that he felt that he should be with them too. I did hate him, then, for embarrassing me, but not enough for me to leave him. We continued in our marriage for three more years. Three more years of his going to them to periodically be a dad to the twins and to try and keep our home intact. Watching him juggle that responsibility and walk the finest of lines, I drew out for him. With me trying to make sure that he paid for his actions left us both miserable. I really have no idea how we became pregnant again, but we did, and after giving birth to our daughter, Alexis, I did close him out. Post-partum depression on top of the regular depression and our mutual embarrassment sealed our fate. I could not forgive him. I shaved my head - my hair was the casualty of my misery. I set my scalp free, while remaining trapped. I only had enough love for our children and not enough for me, and especially not any remaining for him.

"Mercey, will you ever forgive me?" Is what he asked me every morning before he went to work. He asked me that as we sat across the table from each other as our divorce was being written up. He asked me as I signed the contract for divorce. He asked me as he drove away from our home for the last time. I never responded to him. I was too numb. No, I did not think that I could ever forgive him, then.

I look at him now and he asks me again. "Mercey, will you ever forgive me?"

"I have." Finally, I can say that I think that I have. "That is how I am able to be here right now. We are able to co-parent. I, we, have come a long way. We grew up from those sex-crazed kids we were. I am no longer that little girl."

"I know you aren't. I have watched you from a distance."

"Sure, well, I need to go. I am sure that Avery has not fed Aren and Alexis dinner."

"I told him to stop at Alessi's on his way home. I placed the order and gave him the money."

"Why did you do that? What were you planning to have happen here?"

Mock shock plays across his face. "Nothing! Well, something. Maybe, one could hope."

I playfully push him away. I stare at him incredulously.

He cannot be serious.

"I need you. I need us." He is serious.

His raw declaration pulls at me. I swallow, well I try to swallow, but my mouth has become so dry.

"Why now?" I croaked hoarsely.

"I've never stopped needing you."

"So, I am just supposed to let you fill your physical needs with me? Stop it, Alex, you just do not like being alone. I know you!"

"No, not just that, I want it all. That is all of you, all for us. However, I am a man. I will take what you are willing to give me. I need you. You must know that I want all of you."

Somehow, the words cause me to groan. I feel the need rising in me, as he has awakened the beast within. As only Alexander Sterling can, and he knows it.

I stop my mind from reeling. Trying to calculate and recalculate the needs awakening within me. It would feel so good to just this one time allow myself this release. And boy, do I need to RELEASE, R-E-L-E-A-S-E! It has been too long for me. I do not want him to even know that he was my last, physical relationship. It might go to his head. Oh, I came close to going down "pleasure road" with other men; but, each time, I realized that I wanted more than sex - no matter how great or mediocre. I wanted - I want, a relationship. I want a marriage. I want a 50-year anniversary with the love of my lifetime. I want a relationship that GOD HIMSELF would want for me and approved of. The type of relationships that my parents and their parents have had (well, that is before the latest revelation about my paternal grandparents' relationship). I missed that chance with Alexander. Our time has passed, hasn't it? Too much has gotten in the way of my hopes for us. But, here I am standing in his arms, considering adulterous behavior and all because he asked me to. I am considering it. Oh I am so Considering it!

"Please. Please, Mercey let me love you. You know that you want to."

There he goes, reading my mind again. I reason within myself, who would we be hurting? What? I know. I cannot believe that I am considering his proposition either. Betrayed, first by my body and now my mind, but here I am, more turned on than I am offended.

"Umm... We need to be clear about this. With what it

will mean 'if' we do go through with this." No one will get hurt if, again "if", we go about this smartly. I mean, we are too old for games. You know."

I am rambling, I know. Who am I kidding?! In my mind, my pants are being thrown across the room as I speak. My throat is so dry! I look up into Alexander's eyes and I see him smirking at me. Geesh! I collect the glass of wine Alexander sat down on a nearby table for me. I gulp it down. I keep my back to Alexander. It is then, with my new wine- induced courage that I decide 'why not?' I will deal with whatever repercussions, second thoughts and muddled feelings tomorrow. Maybe… maybe just one more time with the marvelous Alexander, then I can go back to my lame ass life. Go back to being the good gal.

I think about the kids. I wonder why they have not called me, especially Alexis. She is a mama's girl, and she has always been overly protective of me. Hey, maybe if she does call me right now, I will have a sign that I should not do this. I pull my phone out my pocket and with one semi-hopeful eye I peek at my screen. Nope. No calls. Not one. Maybe I should call them? I begin to dial my home number when I feel Alexander's arms wrap around my waist. I feel his chest pressing against my back, and I can feel him rising against my behind.

Oohh! Hello Mr. Right now!

"Come on." He takes my cell phone out of my hand. "The kids are fine." He is leading me through the double doors of his master bedroom. More gadgets, more space, more white sterile walls. This is so sad for one person. It seems so lonely. There is a huge king bed on a platform frame. Sprinkled about his room and the bed, for my sake, there are rose petals, the 'beautiful dead'. There is a bottle of champagne on ice, next to the bed, two waiting crystal flutes and a silver platter filled with caviar, toast points, strawberries, olives, and cheese.

"Hmmm. Who were you expecting?" I ask dryly. "Am I really that easy?"

"Who? You? Mercey, no, you were never easy, but one can always hope." His infectious grin has returned, spreading across his mouth. He bends to kiss mine. Familiarity ignites the dormant fires within both of us.

"Ok. Stop!" I am panting trying to regain what little composure I think I still have. "We need to be on the same page with what we both think this is." He lowers his mouth to kiss me again, and I turn my head away as he kisses my neck. "Please, Alex, wait!"

He is unfastening my bra through my blouse. He is making quick work of removing my blouse and bra. His hands now are everywhere. Time has not slowed the artistry of this man's hands & his skills of boundary removal. Determination and feverish desire have taken over. I can see it all in his darkening eyes. I still his hands with my own as he begins to unbutton my jeans, slowing down his singular mission to get me naked. He smiles. He knows my protests are half-hearted and it, (my resistance), is futile. He then decides to humor me.

"Ok." He sighs, "What page should we both settle on? I am making no promises, though."

"This is just a one-time thing. Just tonight. To take the edge off for us both. Simply two friends helping each other out, right? Ok?"

"No."

"No? Why not?"

"No, because I want you back. This cannot be just a one time "thing." I already told you that I want all of you again. I know that I messed that up for us. I am asking that you give me another chance."

"I cannot say that is what I want. THIS IS NOT JUST ABOUT WHAT YOU WANT!!"

"Why? I was kidding when I suggested that we become 'divorced but with benefits'. I seriously want you back."

"All I hear is 'I, I, I!!' This is all about You! You lost 'us' because of YOU! What the FUCK, Alex!! Our messy past exists, too much is there, we cannot recover from it. Yes, 1 won't lie, a good fucking would feel great, but I want more, I need and deserve more. I cannot trust you. This is all too much! Plus, you are STILL A MARRIED MAN!"

"Just on paper."

"That is the tie that binds."

His hands reach out to stroke my exposed nipples. They stiffen at his light touch. He smiles and licks his lips. I forgot that I am half dressed. He whispers, "What are you willing to give me, then? I will try to accept your terms." I groan as he strokes me, and he bends down and sucks my right breast. Oh!

"I, um, I..." I try to focus on my words. I whisper, "Just

tonight. I… Only one time…ooooh…. Once. With no strings. No commitments. No relationship. This is just sex." I think I am telling myself this more than I am saying it to him.

"So, to be clear, you are suggesting that I only have tonight to change your mind about taking me back?"

I open my mouth to respond, and he claims my mouth with his.

The rest of my clothes are now a pile on the floor as he explores my body with his hands and mouth. I am barely able to remain standing, my knees have weakened, and desire has taken my strength. He stops his exploration, he walks over to the champagne, and he pours it into the crystal flutes. His eyes never leave mine. I look at his mouth and I want it to continue it's assault, devouring me and my inhibitions. I want to cover myself. My soon to be 40-year old stomach, thighs and breasts are not as firm as they once were. I want to shield them from his gaze, keeping him from seeing my "problem areas." I begin to bring my arms up to cover myself, and he says, "Don't."

I ask, "Don't what?"

"Do not cover yourself." Damn him, ever the mind

reader!

"Look," I say, "I am not the 18-year-old track-star, hell, I am not even the 28-year-old you remember. I am 38 and things are a lot different now on this body!"

"Hey! You are the one who said that I only have this one night, so I am going to memorize every curve since that is what I will have to live with for the rest of my life."

Is that sarcasm reflecting in his voice? Who does he think he is kidding? The rest of his life? Yeah right. I reply, "I do not think that you have enough memory for all of this! I am like 30 lbs. overweight and right now, I am feeling every pound and inch of it!"

"I like it. Your once hard body is now softer and fuller. In all the right places. It looks good on you. It feels good to me."

I drink, not sip, the champagne he has just handed me. "You still have on all of your clothes. I am feeling underdressed for this party."

"I will let you remedy that. Drink this first." He hands me his flute of champagne and takes my empty one from my hands. He aims a remote in the air and music begins to play. Prince's voice is slow and soulful, singing our song "Insatiable." He remembered. Once again, I tilt back the glass of champagne. It is good. So good, but my nerves will not let me savor it. I am still standing naked here and he keeps drinking in the view. I walk over to the champagne bottle and pour myself the third glass determined to drink/sip this one a lot slower and I see that it is Ace of Spades. Such a trendy, super pricey champagne, but I would not expect anything else from Alexander. I ask him, "Nothing less than the best, right?" I arched my brows at him. He shrugs.

"I can only say that the best is you."

I gulp down the third glass just like the previous two and the glass of wine before that. I am not sure if I had enough to eat to soak up this much libations. I pick up a piece of cheese and spoon a little caviar on a toast point. All while nibbling and trying to keep my posture and hold in my stomach at the same time. My eyes drift around the room and my gaze rests on his bed. He wants me on his bed. This bed he shared with her?! What the hell am I doing? Am I crazy?! He catches my gaze, and he senses my change in mood.

"What is wrong.? What happened?"

"I cannot do this, Alex. Not here, and NOT there!" I point to his bed. When did I become so dramatic? I guess when it comes to her… I just want nothing to do with her, at all.

"What, the bed? It is a new bed. When I said that she took everything, I meant it - She. Took. Everything! As a matter of fact, you will be this bed's maiden voyage."

"Oh." I flush and say as I drink another glass of champagne. I really should slow down. I am losing count, and I will not even enjoy the tryst, and there will be one, if I continue drinking like this.

He walks over to me and reaches for a strawberry. He places the strawberry in my mouth. I barely have time to taste it when he begins kissing me again. Greedily we share the strawberry with both of our mouths fighting to take down the sweet juicy fruit exchange. Butterflies begin to jump around in my stomach. I am really enjoying the playfulness we are sharing. The schoolgirl in me is ready to take over the now mature woman I have become. I begin to giggle. I giggle at us and how we are right now. I attempt another giggle and a throaty moan and chuckle hybrid escapes from my throat. Nope, mature Mercey is still here, she refuses to surrender completely to this encounter.

I realize, again, he is still fully clothed as I reach my arms around his neck. I begin to unbutton his oxford, and I unbutton his cuffs and slide his shirt off. I run my hands over his chest he still has on an undershirt, but I can feel his hard body underneath. No fair! He is much leaner than I remember, much more muscular than before. I remember him always having an athletic build, but this is more, so much more! My hands move to his arms, and I am not disappointed, muscles there abound. "You have been working out." I mutter in between kisses.

"Um hmm." He mumbles.

Our lips part as I pull his undershirt over his head. It is then I am able to see exactly what he has been up to at the gym. Oh, I very much like what I am seeing. Forty is FABULOUS! Now, I want to run two laps after seeing him and his hot toned body. He is so much more than what I remember. The last few years have been good for him. Me likely. I unbutton his pants and slide them down. Abs? He has abs still! My God he has the "V." That Adonis belt is tight!

As I move my hands across his waist and down, I grip his boxers and I feel his rock-hard ass and his smooth and silky skin, he has hair in just the right places.

Magnificence one must see for themselves. I want to taste him and see if he is as sweet as he looks. Chocolate and caramel are all I can think of as I look at him. I see his manhood is throbbing, pulsating, with his every breath or heartbeat. It bobs, beckoning me to hurry up. Like a horse, waiting at the gate, ready for the race to begin. I hate when people refer to men as animals, but here Alexander stands, and I can see the simile as a magnificent chestnut Akhal-Teke stallion. I see the beauty of the vision. He is a magnificent beast. My eyes widen with anticipation. My wetness flows as if a dam has broken. I am so ready. I know that no matter how much, mentally, I will try to make myself regret this night, I know physically, I never will.

I kneel down to help him remove his clothes, and as he steps out of his pants, my 'special friend' hits me on top of my head. We laugh. Alejandro has come out to say hello to Mercia. These are the pet names we gave to our lesser selves. I touch him, run my hand up his thickening shaft. He moans. I know his buttons, too. He whispers, "I have missed your touch. Only you can touch me, and I feel it deep within." Soon, our hands are everywhere. Exploring each other, taking in what is familiar and what is new. He groans as he reaches in between my legs, he feels my welcome. We look into each other's eyes. The intensity has clouded his it is then that I know he has reached the point, that point of no return. We would not be able to stop even if we wanted to. We both fall onto the bed, still reaching, searching, and kissing. He removes my hair clip so that he can play in my wavy curls.

"I like that you have gone natural, and that you let it grow long. It really suits you," he whispers. He grabs a handful of hair and pulls my head back. He kisses my throat, neck, and clavicle.

I laugh and say a throaty, "Thanks. I am glad you like it." He pulls a nipple into his mouth and begins to suck it greedily and he repeats the same on the other side. He is the fat kid in a candy store.

I feel him reach over to the table near his bed as he still is ministering to my breasts. He pulls a condom package out and I grab it. I open it and place it on him. I have to feel Alejandro again. He is so, oh! I take great care not to damage the condom with my nails. As I slide it down his shaft I stare into his eyes. I position him outside my gates. I breathe in deeply and relax my muscles and he slides in. Home.

At first, I feel awkward and clumsy, like I am rushing,

I am too eager. It has been too long for me, and I am overthinking my moves. After a few more strokes, our hips create the graceful rhythm we always had. But, somehow, this is new. With each thrust, he fills me with a surge of energy. My senses are heightened and every fiber of my being is raging. I give to him, and he gives to me. With each stroke we meet each other until the urgent ecstasy arrives. I wrap my legs around him, taking in all of him, craving all of him. He is at work, executing the task of sending me into orbit. He knows every one of my spots and he is a master at their command. He spins his magic, and I am caught up in his spell. He signs his name within me again, I have been Signed, Sealed and Delivered.

We collapse on the bed; exhausted and spent. Or, so I thought, we both were. I know that I was.

But after holding me in his embrace for what seemed like only five minutes, he grins and says, "What did you say again? I only had one shot or was it that we only had one night, tonight? Well, the night is still young."

"Hmmmm?" I purr. I cannot speak because my head and my mouth were left somewhere near Mars. He cannot be serious. What was his question, again?

"What?"

He began kissing my stomach. He was moving lower. "Did you say that I only had one time with you, or was it that we had only tonight?" He kisses my inner thigh. "I need to know. If we are to be only for tonight, then I am ready for round two."

"Excuse me?"

He kisses the other thigh, and he starts to kiss his way towards Mercia. He teases her with his tongue. "Round two is about to begin."

"Wait! Hold on a minute. I still have yet to recover from round one, it is still claiming me as we speak. How can you be ready so fast? Are you taking performance enhancing drugs, or something?"

"No, babe, I have everything that I need, right here." He licks Mercia again. I soar higher. "What I am going to take is a little more of Mercia, though." With that he takes "her" into his mouth. His tongue is notarizing what documents Alejandro signed moments before. Butterflies take over, more of those damned butterflies. The flutters take over my stomach and I begin to spasm. I cannot stifle the surges that overtake me. The moans escape my mouth so rapidly. I cannot hold back my gasps. I cannot catch my breath as he sends me back into the outer limits of space and time. I squeal. I think I even scream, but he does not stop. I feel him smile and I hear him laugh, but he does not stop the rhythm he is making. Once again, he has become the fat kid at the candy store, with no budget, no limit, and no line at checkout. No limits, Bill Gates, Warren Buffet, Elon Musk, Jeff Bezos style.

He reaches for another condom, and he never breaks his stride he comes up from the dive and in the same smooth motion Alejandro is inside Mercia. Like surfers, we ride each wave he is creating. I had barely opened my eyes from the first, and now here is the second cuming. I am cuming so fast and so hard. How is this happening to me? Fireworks explode in my ears. Can he hear them, too? I only left this moment in my head for a second. I began to rearrange my schedule for the upcoming week, hell, weeks. I had to come back for more. Alexander has done it again. Oh, I am so dick-whipped, and I don't even care. IDGAF.

After round four (or was it five?) I had to get up and leave for home. He whined for me to stay with him, but I had to get back to the kids. I had to leave Fantasy Island and return to reality. I was beginning to want what we just made a part of my real world. I was having crazy & wild thoughts. As I prepared to make my private "walk of shame" to my SUV at 2 AM, he grabs my hand, kisses my palm, and says, "Thank you."

'Thank you'? Who says 'Thank you' after what we just did? He makes it sound as if we just completed a business transaction. I murmur "Mmm hmm." That is all that I can think of to respond. Although my knees are still weak, I continue walking shakily to my Mercedes SUV, and he opens the door for me.

"I wish that you could stay longer," he said. Again, another odd statement from him, but whatever.

I whispered, "No" as I buckled my seatbelt. He closes the door. By the time I straighten myself up, I looked around and he is already retreating through his front door. As he turned off the outside lights, I questioned 'what just happened'? No lingering goodbyes, no additional kisses? Just like that? The session is over. Foolish Mercedes, I chastise myself as I drive home.

Six hours ago, he was whispering "I love you's". Now there is nothing. No call. Not one eff-ing call! Emotionally, I feel used and dirty. Physically, I feel satisfied, but still! Now, I remember why I chose celibacy. It is because of the morning after. There is no one beside me in this bed or no one to whisper "good morning" to. Just the ghostly memories of the night before lingering about in my head. Excitement at the thought of the act(s), then the letdown once they are over. Mourning the acts of love as they become a part of the past. Like Christmas Day, it is over too soon; without there being a relationship, the uncertainty that it may or may not happen again, and the wanting for it to happen again, and again (AND AGAIN!).

Now it is the day after, and he still has not called. You wrote a check that you did not want him to cash, I think to myself. Wasn't it you told him 'no strings, no commitment'? Then why are you mad he accepted your terms? Twelve hours ago, when you were being ridden and you riding him, you allowed yourself to dream of more, of having a future with Alex, but you did not let him in on the dream. Even if it seems like it at times, he is not actually a mind reader. If you expected more, then when did you communicate it to him? What you assumed by his sweet, impassioned words of longing was that he would decide that he could not - no, that he would not be able to honor the terms of your agreement? Grow the fuck up Mercey. Men will say anything to get into your panties, especially when you are standing in front of them, acting unsure. Such is the chase all men love, an easy gazelle for the Lion King.

I was too embarrassed to go to church after last night's activities. I fictionalized that somehow the Spirit of GOD would inform everyone of what I was up to. A still quiet whisper of "she's been fornicating" and "there's the adulteress" played in my mind. I then heard my mother's voice from when I was a child, "Do not do it, if you will be ashamed or embarrassed when or if, you are found out." I chuckled at myself for my silly imaginations, but still I remained in bed. I resigned myself to feeling guilty but satisfied; and, I "chalked this one up to the game," and I decided to take another shower.

After finishing my long shower, I emerged from the master bathroom to see our bubbly eleven-year old daughter bouncing on my bed. Alexis seems so small in the huge four poster king sized bed monstrosity I sleep in every night, alone.

"Mommy, why didn't we go to church today? You did not wake us up. I was supposed to sing in Kid's Praise!"

Shoot! I forgot! "I am sorry, sweetie. I was up very late last night."

"Were you with daddy?" She giggles.

"Yes, and why are you giggling?"

"Oh, it's nothing. He told us that he and you needed to "talk." (Yes, she holds up her little hands and does air quotes). What she means by that I have no idea. I wonder if she even knows. "He was cooking dinner and I got to help him. I was his assistant. Ummm, I washed the strawberries, and I plucked the petals off of a lot of roses… What's wrong, mama?"

She must have seen the dread that had taken over my face. I was never able to hide what I was thinking. The last thing I wanted to talk to my daughter about was the night I spent with her father. Hearing how he used our daughter to help him prepare his seduction plans was too much! What's next? Will I learn that he asked Avery and/or Aren to go pick up his condoms?

"Uh, nothing, baby. Those roses weren't for me" I lied. Hey, after everything else I have done recently just add it to the list. I reason it was not a complete lie, though. In retrospect, they were not exactly for me, they were really for Mercia. His goal was to get into my pants for her. So there. What is even sadder is if he were to call me right now, all would be forgiven.

Alexis is chattering as all eleven-year-olds do. She is our princess and she is excited for and about everything in her life. The world is her oyster, and her father and I are the pearl divers. Avery is taking her to her best friend Amber's "Super 12-year Blast!" A birthday/end of the school year/pool/slumber party. According to Alexis and her friends, summer has never officially begun, until Amber's party. Even if school has been out for two weeks already. "Amber's party is the official 'jump off', mama", Alexis explains to me as she gives me an exasperated sigh and rolls her eyes up at me.

I pretend to 'tune in' to Alexis' chatter, but honestly it has really just become white noise to the chaos brewing inside of my mind. What is Alexander thinking? Is he testing me, or is he really ok with last night being a onetime thing? Maybe in the morning light, he has decided that I was right about us, and that he dodged another bullet with me. Or is he waiting for me to call him? That's it. He wants to see if I will stick to the terms that I created for us. Is this a game of chicken? Surely, he does not expect me to call him - could he? I pick up the phone. I put it back down. I will not, I cannot, call him.

I know I will call my sisters, IsaMara and Maria. No, I cannot tell them that I have been with Alex. They will think that I am crazy! I know, I will call Letricia, my best friend, she can offer some insight. I hear Alexis say that she is going to eat breakfast, and she kisses me on the cheek. The interruption only distracts my thoughts briefly and then I begin to think more disturbing thoughts like maybe Raemier came back. What if he is taking her back right now? She was the one who left him, right? Oh, my dear GOD! An adulterous vixen, that is what I have become. Ugh! I can hear the universe laughing at me! I am so pathetic. Who cares?! They weren't "together" when we were, and so what she has done to me is far worse. Damn that man! I am going too far with all of this. I am assuming a lot with no information. I am letting my imagination run away from me. I need to just calm down and breathe. It is what it is, no more, no less. I realize that I have been squeezing the hell out of my phone's handset and now my hand has begun to ache. I shake my head at myself and whisper, "You poor and foolish, oh, and horny girl!"

Resisting the urge to crawl back into bed and sink deeply under my duvet, I pick up my imagined shame and walk down the stairs into my tiny world - where I find my children.

I am not surprised. All three are eating breakfast

around the massive granite slab that serves as the kitchen island and breakfast bar. There they are, my beautiful daughter and my two handsome young men. Alexis with her long dark brown curls is a beautiful budding young lady. Woe to the young man who woos her heart. Then we have Avery, 16 years, and Aren, 13 years, each one a hybrid of me and Alexander. Avery, who seems to be growing every day, stands at 5' 11." He has an athletic build, thanks to the daily conditioning and weightlifting regimen his coaches and dad have him on. He is a star on Plant High School's basketball and football teams, and he is aiming for state and national recognition. On top of all of that, he is smart and is a tech and science geek. Avery was always taking some small gadget apart and reconstructing it, it began when he was a small child. Now, he loves to take something apart and improve it as he puts it back together. He also constructs his own creations and is the co-captain of the robotics team at school. I see MIT banging on our door in the not-too-distant future.

Aren is 5' 9" and although he is sometimes an athlete, meaning he likes to workout with his dad and older brother; and is on the basketball and track & field team at his middle school, is truly a mama's boy, and my poet and musician. He plays classical piano and the Spanish Acoustic guitar. He loves to sing, and his voice sends the schoolgirls into a frenzy. The girls, oh, those silly teenage girls, are always sashaying past my boys whenever we are out. What are their mothers not teaching them? They are shameless in their pursuits to gain the Sterling boys' attention. I have Alex constantly talking to them about protection and how an STD or an unwanted pregnancy can derail and maybe even ruin their lives. I am constantly on them about being respectful, how they should behave, and for them to stay focused. There will always be time for girls. I am constantly telling them about choosing the right, confident young lady who respects herself as well as them. Also, telling them how to protect themselves and to not get "caught up" in the physical and superficial romances of teenage life. I have horror stories, some even are personal ones that I am ready to divulge if necessary. Avery has had a steady girlfriend, Brianna, for a year. Aren has a steady stream of desperate girls. I do not think either of them realize how cute they are. They think that all of this attention is normal. They are their father's children. I shake my head at the thought. Although, since they have become teenagers, it is proving to be difficult to control the hormones bouncing all over this place. Much to my chagrin, although, we are not giving him permission to have sex, Alex insisted that Avery carry condoms in his wallet. He reasoned that it is better to be safe than sorry. If Avery decides to do it, there is nothing that we can do about it. Hey! Maybe that is my problem. Their hormones have been affecting me! That sounds good! That's it! Horny hormones have been jumping from them to me and their dad. That must be it.

"Hey mom!" Aren said, jolting me out of my thoughts.

"Hey mom! Did you have a good time last night?" Avery inquired.

"What? Why? Huh?" I'm startled by his question.

"With dad, I mean he said that you were going to play Trivial Pursuit so you can unwind. I told him how stressed you were lately. With your finals and all that he is going through with Rae, you both could use the break. I hope that was ok for me to mention?"

"Yeah, sure that was ok." I sigh, "It was ok. I mean, you know, for you to have mentioned it." I sigh at myself again. Honey, you are pathetic.

"Mom, are you ok?" Aren asks me.

No, son, I am not ok! I think to myself. Now, all eyes are on me. I just smile at my children who are now looking at me so worriedly. Then just like that, they go back to their thing. Alexis starts to ungracefully stuff cereal into her mouth. Aren begins texting whoever his latest chica is. Avery begins drinking his protein shake again, but he keeps his eyes on me a little longer. I smile at him again. "Yes, honey, I am fine." I rub his cheek. More lies. I turn to go back to my room. My appetite is gone. I just need to regroup again.

CHAPTER 2

Monday. Over 24 hours ago, I was a wanton woman. Did I kill Alex? I knew it! He must have taken a "blue pill" for that stamina he exhibited Saturday night! He probably had a heart attack. Maybe I should send Lo, Alex's twin brother, over to check on him? I knew that we were going at it too hard! I knew he was sweating too much. I killed him! Death by sex. Am I wrong if I am glad that he did not die on top of me? Too messy. Too horrible to ponder any longer, I pick up the phone to call Alex, I am letting my imagination run wild again. I have to know what is up.

I have the handset to my ear, but I do not hear a dial tone. I say into the phone's mouthpiece, "Hello?"

"Hey." It is him. I can hear the smirk in his voice.

"The children called me this morning they said that you were in your bed all day yesterday and I am told that you still are. Did I put it on you that good?"

"I was picking up the phone to call you. I thought that I killed you. You know since I have not heard from you." I reply.

He chuckles. "That would not be a bad way to go. But seriously, you are ok, aren't you?"

So many emotions rise to the surface. Anger, embarrassment and oh, excitement. What, excited? Really? Seriously, body, stay with me! I clear my throat. "Umm, yeah, I am fine. Just a little headache from the wine and champagne and, uh, the extra excitement and activities." Eh-hum, I clear my throat again.

"Oh."

I then ask, "Why haven't you called me before now?"

"Did you want me to?"

"Well, not so much as want, but I did expect you to." I lied, I wanted him to call.

"Interesting. Why didn't you call me? I thought that you said there will be no games, strings, or commitments. The last time I had that kind of situation, it is called a booty call by the way, so calling the next day is not necessary. Just the call for the next rendezvous, which happens if the first encounter was satisfactory. And the encounter was satisfying. These were your terms, remember?"

"Yes, I remember." I feel like the naughty schoolgirl talking to her history professor.

"So?"

What does he expect for me to say?

"The reason why I am calling is to ask if you and the kids would come over."

"Just like that, huh? Are we on to the next subject?"

"Yes, just like that."

"Well, Avery and Aren went to the park to play

basketball and Alexis is still over at Amber's house. Remember the slumber party she has been talking about for months if not, days?"

"Well, that leaves one of you who is free. What are you doing today? Come over?"

"No, I have to do…"

"Me."

"Excuse me?"

"I was finishing your sentence. You have to do 'Me'. Come on over, you know that you want to. You have beaten yourself up enough about Saturday. Now it is time to add some more events to the list. I do not know why you are upset; I had a great time and I thought that it was mutual. No regrets, remember? My ego is beginning to get injured now that I am finding that you have some. That is not what I wanted for our reunion. Let me make it better for you."

"hmmm, how can you do that? I wonder."

"Come on over, and I'll show you."

"Oh Yeah? I forgot to thank you."

"Thank me? Thank me for what?"

"Yes, Thank you. Like when you thanked me the other day as if you were thanking a paid hooker for getting you off. Oh, and do not forget the "ole, I wish you could stay longer" as you are running back inside to your bed. Real nice touch!"

"I knew that was going to bother you as soon as those words left my mouth. You will have to forgive me, my brain was low on oxygen and blood, plus I do not think that my synapses were firing well enough for intelligent conversations. I was putting in some heavy work, you know!" He is laughing at me.

"Well, I guess you are right. You were working it." I laugh at myself. "I have been celibate for years and you ended that in a matter of minutes. I am ashamed of myself. This whole situation will not work for me. I am just … I am just too cerebral for casual relationships."

"I know that you are. Let's not be casual."

"What do you mean?"

"Let me show you."

"I cannot. I do not want just a physical relationship."

"A what? That is not what I am suggesting. Are you afraid? Just come over. I will see you in 20 minutes, ok?"

"NO."

"Why not? I have something that I need for you to see. If you do not come over here, I will come over there."

"No. Don't!"

"Well, then come over here, Mercey. Don't make me beg. I will beg you, but don't require it from me. My ego, you know, it is already fragile." I hear the feigned wounded sounds he is attempting to convey.

"Boy, you are silly."

"Yes, I am, is it helping?"

I laugh, "Apparently."

"Good come over here, Mercey. It will take you about 20 minutes, right?"

"No."

"No, you aren't coming or that you need more like 30 minutes?"

"No, that I will only need 15 minutes."

"Ohhhhh Yes, I like that!"

Ms. Dick-whipped times 70!

When I pull up to his home, Alexander is waiting for me in his courtyard. His smile is beaming, fully "on." He has the most radiant smile. It lights up his entire face and body. His smile seems to ebb up from his insides and it is infectious. He is rarely without his smile. It is security, and at times it is his weapon. Even when he sat across from me at our divorce mediation, he reassured me with his smile, trying to convince me that everything will eventually be well again. Now, here we are, things are better between us. Wow, his world must be a great place to live. It has to be, because here I am again.

He opens the door to my SUV.

"Hello beautiful."

Wait. What is this? Am I blushing?

"Hello handsome." I laugh at myself, for feeling so giddy. I then ask him, "Why are you beaming?" He really is beaming at me.

"I am glad that you are here."

Taking my hand, I step out of the SUV. He shuts the door behind me, and he places a kiss on my lips. He leads me indoors, through his house to his lanai in the rear of his home. There is a tropical paradise in front of me. Waterfalls surround a rock and boulder lagoon style pool with a grotto hot spa. Palm trees, birds of paradise, a canopy of more flora and fauna float above us all underneath a huge bronze colored cage screened enclosure. This is such a huge departure from the ultra-modern home, but not a huge departure from Alex and his need to have the biggest and best of everything. It dawns on me how foreign Alex's house is to me. I rarely went inside his home when I dropped off the children to him; and I never went past the foyer, that is, prior to Saturday. I look around, taking in the spectacle. Appreciating the small touches and taking notes for my own backyard. I like the theme he has, and then I remember where I have seen this scene before. He recreated our honeymoon. It is Fiji in his backyard. We discovered a smallish waterfall and lagoon on a walk we took on one of the few days we left our hotel. I do not know how he did this, because I am almost certain we did not take a camera with us. But here it is, our Fiji paradise. So many thoughts begin to surface, as I am interrupted by his voice.

"Hungry?"

It is then that I see his set up. He has a table with 3 fondue pots. Each one filled with something different; one is filled with bubbling hot oil, another with cheese, and the last has chocolate. Next to the pots there are platters filled with skewers of crusty breads, soft breads, chunky meat, apple wedges, pineapples, strawberries, and marshmallows and graham crackers. He remembers my smores fascination.

"You like to feed me, huh?"

"Yes, it is sexy to feed my love, mentally, spiritually, and physically."

"You may do that, possibly 2 out of the 3. I do not think that we feed each others' spiritual needs. Especially with me missing church yesterday! I had so much guilt about our fornicating and adulterous behavior!" I try to muster my best old Southern church lady voice.

"Well, I do not know about all that, but you sure called on Jesus enough for it to be considered a spirit-filled experience!"

"I did not, Blasphemer!" We both laugh.

"Well, let me ease the "guilt" so that you will no more feel the role of an adulterer. I was going to wait until later, but here since you brought it up." He slides a long manila folder over to me, "Here, look at this."

I open the folder and pull out its contents. It is a divorce decree. I am holding in my hands his and Raemier's divorce. It was signed by both of them yesterday. "Has this been filed, yet?" Please say yes! Wait, do I really want this for my sake? Why do you care, Mercey? Oh gee, girl, get it together!

"Yes, I had Lorenzo file it today. That is my copy."

"So, Lo knows about this already? So, you are a single man, again."

"Yes, ma'am! Just waiting for the finalization, and you are here to help me celebrate!"

"Are you sure that this is really what you want? At the risk of sounding very vain in this moment, you did not do this for me, did you? Because I am not ready to …" There he goes again, kissing my sentences away. His kiss is gentle, not greedy, hungry nor is it pawingly animalistic like Saturday. He grazes my lips with his.

This kiss is delicate, but is still possessive, a confident ownership.

I am melting into him all over again. This is definitely a chemical and physical response. I am drawn to him. Like a moth to the flame. My body has been craving him for years, like someone starving and not realizing it until they are sitting at a buffet. I feel partially complete again, but not in my heart and mind, sirens are blaring in my ears and my gut is screaming "Nooo!" Which is an old familiar feeling, one that I have squelched so many times before. I open my eyes in this kiss, and I see him looking at me. Our eyes meet, and although I know it's a cliché, (but it is my truth), I feel our souls are connected again. I feel it, sparks, new and the old colliding. My senses are awakening. This cannot really be love? Is it? It is sad, for me that I really, honestly do not know what it is to be "in love."

I feel his hands raising my sundress over my head, and then with no resistance, my bra and panties are next. I am standing there, naked, with only my espadrille sandals on my feet. Here we are again, me naked and him drinking me in. Me left exposed and Alex taking control and making it easier for him to remove my boundaries so that I will let him in, easily. Him confusing physical boundaries with emotional ones, but not really, because it has been effective thus far.

"Let's go for a swim." he says.

"Right, now?" He is bending down to remove my sandals. He gently lifts my left, and then my right foot to remove them.

"Yes, right now." He picks up a remote and Sade begins to sing soulfully "Smooth Operator", if only she really knew how smoothie he is.

I let him lead me to the edge of the pool where there is a 0° beach-like entry. The water temperature is not too cold nor too warm. Just like that day in Fiji, it is perfect. He removes my hair clip.

"I love your hair." He whispers. He grazes the nape of my neck with his lips. He removes his clothes, and we walk to where the water is chest deep for me. He pulls me close to him. He lowers his head to whisper, "So, why didn't you call me yesterday?" I do not answer him. "Did you want to call me? Was pride preventing your call?" I still do not repond to his probing. He lifts my chin. I look up into his eyes. Again, I am drawn into him. Our souls were colliding, connecting, and then separating, melding, and pulling away. I listen to his heartbeat, "I will not pretend here, I want us together again. If that is not what you think you want, tell me. I will wait for you to change your mind." I open my mouth to finally respond, but he stops me. "You do not have to reply right now. By your being here, it gives me hope."

I shake my head. I sink into the water, leaving his embrace to actually swim. I swim to clear my head. I swim to break from his familiar smell, to break the pheromone overload that muddles my senses. To break his spell. I want to be honest with him. I must be honest with myself. I am enjoying myself with him, but I do not know if I want to give him 'hope.' I simply just do not know what I want. This man standing here holding me is so familiar, yet so different, changed, but the same. Is he the same boy who hurt my soul for years, asking me for another chance? For what purpose? Is it that he does not know how to be alone? Do I honestly have more to give him? I forgave him because we aren't, or weren't, connected any more. This is the kind of forgiveness for the sake of continuity and peace. Can I forgive him for the past in the context of us being reunited? Thus, truly forgetting everything? My deep depressions all caused my family to have suffered. I am left deeply wounded from my disappointments and from his selfishness. Then, I had the breakdown, or should I say breakdowns. I just shut everyone out the day that he walked away from us. A lot of prayer, counseling, antidepressants (which left me numb) - I tried everything.

If it were not for my mother's 'tough love', I do not know where I would be. She threatened to take my children from me. I can still hear her voice, "Mercedes, if you do not get it together, your father and I are taking the children. I am not punishing you, but they deserve more than what you are giving them, right now. Forget Alex, he is the fool, do not be one, too!" Words, they have a way of shaking things up and breaking through to the core. I would not give her cause to carry out her threat. I began to get my life together that very moment. Pulling myself up at times, but it was always by Divine appointment that I came to be free. I stopped taking the antidepressants and sleeping medications. I realized that to find myself, I had to feel again. I was taking antidepressants for all the wrong reasons. I enrolled in martial arts classes and crafting classes, to give myself an outlet for creativity. I noticed that I was most happy being creative. I especially enjoyed the pottery classes. I also enrolled in a few courses at our local community college, in attempts to try to decide what path I would like to take. I am still undecided, but the classes are fun. It took the better part of a year for me to recover. At times, I feel that I may not still be completely recovered. Based on my latest behavior, this may be my normal. I question whether I am choosing to get back into my loop of what feels normal to me. I wonder if I am seeking a little (or a lot) of validation from his feelings of remorse.

I know him. At least, I think that I do. He always knows exactly what to say, for every situation. He reads people and behaviors for a living. He especially knows how to read me. I have shed a lot of tears for and because of him. If I take him back, will there be more tears in my future? Who knows? If I were not standing here, would there be a possibility that I would want or even consider taking him back? He is intoxicating to me. Is this why I am considering reuniting with him? I am not sure of what it is that I want, at all. Am I chasing the fairy tale or is this what I truly think I want? I do not think that Alex has any idea what it is he is asking of me. I am most definitely not the same silly little girl he knew before; no not anymore. Plus, by my sisters' tone yesterday, I think my family will disown me if I did take him back so quickly; if at all. I do not live my life for anyone, but I cannot deny it would hurt me if anyone I love would be less than happy for me. And, what would our children think? They are finally used to us being separated. Would they want us to reunite? Who knows?

My leisurely swim has been so focused on my thoughts, that I really have forgotten where I was. I am brought back to reality by his voice which startles me.

"What are you thinking about so intently, Mercey?" Was he just watching me swim back and forth and floating all this time? I have always been able to shut things out really well which comes from having 4 other siblings.

"I love your pool, Alex. How were you able to bring Fiji here?" Yes, I avoided his question, so what?

He chuckles, "So, you noticed that, huh?"

"Yes, I did." Floating on my back, I intentionally place my breasts in the air, the cool air causes my nipples to harden. I open my eyes to see his reaction. Yep! His eyes are drawn to them. Are they not too bad for 38 years? I think not.

He walks closer to me. He reaches for my breasts, and he begins to stroke each nipple absent-mindedly. "Well, that is a funny story. I went back to Fiji after our divorce, to think and clear my head. I had been looking for that lagoon for two days, and I was about to give up. Then, one day, I blew a tire on my bike, and, since, I was not far from the hotel; I started to walk and that is when I stumbled upon an overgrown path in an area that looked familiar. I heard the waterfall and then I saw it in a clearing, I was on the opposite bank, and I had to walk around to get back to the area we discovered that day. I took so many pictures and I had my architect recreate 'our spot' here when I built this home."

"Does Raemier know that?"

"Are you kidding me? No, but she left the design up to me. I just had to promise to not use any designs influenced by our home. Thus, you see this modern marvel is far from the old-world charm of our home."

"Our home?"

"Sorry, your home." He sighs at me; I smirk at him. "Anyway, what have you been thinking about? You ignored me for over a half hour."

"I was thinking about what you said earlier. It is not a light statement, and I seriously do not think that you understand what you are asking of me."

"I do know exactly what I am asking."

"No, I do not think that you do. My family had to go through hell to get me back on track after you left us. You left me broken and depressed. My reality was damaged and broken. After Alexis, the post-partum depression was a nightmare and on top of it all you left me to manage it all alone."

He looks wounded, his smile has faded. "I thought that I was there for you, Mercey. You shut me out. You did not want me anymore."

"Then you should have broken through. You should have done everything and anything you needed to break through and not let me go. Cling to me because you needed me to be well. No, instead you left me. You left us!" Damn it, here the tears come pouring out. He lifts me up and holds me tight. I try to break free from his embrace, but he held me tighter.

"I will now, if you will let me."

"I do not know if I can be who you are asking me to be. It could be too late."

"Don't say that."

"I will not play games with you, and I will not give

you false hope. That is probably why, I did not call you yesterday. I am really not sure what I want from you. This is not just about us, this is our children's lives, our families, and they may not want "us" either."

"You know, I never lived my life for what I felt or even knew, what other people wanted. Besides, I already asked them."

"What?! Who? Who did you ask?"

"I already talked to our kids. I asked them how they would feel about us possibly reconciling. Saturday, before you came over, I told them that I was still in love with you. I asked them to forgive me for what I did wrong to our family. Then, I asked them how they would feel about us getting back together. Aren and Alexis were excited, but you know Avery, he was not 100% sure. He asked me about Raemier and how it would affect her, Adrian, and Andre."

"You should not have involved them without me. We should have asked them together after serious discussion as to whether it was something we both wanted."

"It is something I want; and, I know, if I can prove that I will not hurt you, you will want it too. I have to prove myself to you again."

"That is very selfish of you, Alex. This is not all about what you want, and what you think I want. The children do not need to know anything about "us" at this point. They should not have any expectation of us getting back together right now. I do not want to have to disappoint them if we are not, in fact, getting back together."

"Please come back here." I realized that I had pried myself from him and that I was wading away from him. I stopped in front of him. Then it dawned on me, by my staying in bed, deeply underneath the covers, my poor children may have thought I was drifting into another depression this past Sunday. Geesh! The POOR Things!

"So, what did they say when they called you?" I ask.

He reaches for me again, I back away, but he grabs my hands before I am completely out of his reach. He interlocks our fingers. Electricity! I immediately shoot down my instant arousal. I remind myself it is only a physical reaction. It is only our chemistry. Even so, I feel it there, bubbling underneath. Reaching out to him from my core, my body saying, screaming no at me, "Fuck you, Mercey, we want him!"

"They asked me 'what did I do to you'?" He chuckles, "Imagine the conversation had I told them what really went down between us." I chuckle too, yeah imagine that. "I just asked them why they were asking, and Aren said that you had been in bed all day. I told you that already." I must have had a concerned look on my face.

"Aren was the one who called you?"

"Yes, but I think that the other two put him up to it, because they put me on speaker when I answered."

"They probably thought that I was depressed again."

"No, I do not think so. However, they probably did think that I disappointed you again, thoug which would be the more logical expectation. Especially, when they consider it is me."

He pulls me in closer to him. He lifts our interlocked hands and places my arms around his neck. My breasts are up against his chest. The heat is intense. We hold each other. Because of the water, I am slightly weightless in his embrace. His hands rub up and down the small of my back. We sway rhythmically to Raheem Devaughn. I know that this music mix is for me. He loves rap. T-Pain is probably the slowest artist on his personal playlist. I remember the days when he would shut his home office doors to prepare for trading, he would crank up his volume and turn on, what I called, his "war cries." Rappers rapping about a lifestyle which he did not know. His upper-upper class upbringing did not help him understand what it meant to be that destitute, neither did I for that matter. I would laugh at his sincere recitals of the downtrodden. He would say that he did not have to experience the roughest of times to know that it was not for him. His parents were wealthy, and they made no apologies for providing the best for their children, and he would do the same for his family. Our dancing moves to playful splashing and swimming, intermittent touching/groping sessions and then to some semiserious handstand competitions which, of course, Alex wins. He leads me into his grotto hot tub, and we talk about lighter and airier subjects, something to keep us lighter and airier. No more heavy thoughts, no more weighted discussions required for today. Just being here in the now, the present is where we want to exist.

Later, we are sitting back at the table eating the delicious fondue he prepared. We are laughing at some vague memory he brought up. I realize that I am happy here in this place with Alex. Yes, I can admit that I am comfortable and blissfully happy. I am warm in the fluffy robes he brought out for us to put on.

"Thank you for skinny-dipping with me and joining me in my celebration."

"You are welcome. I'm having a great time here."

"I want you to celebrate every celebration with me from now on."

I shift in my seat. I am uncomfortable with him planning my future. "Thank you, that sounds promising, but…"

Then, at that very moment Lorenzo, Alex's twin brother, walks through the door. Lorenzo is about one inch shorter than Alexander and a little thinner, and a lot more intense. He does not have Alex's ease, or the fully practiced relaxed charisma or Alex's charm. His is more of a nerd.

"Damn dawg, you cannot pick up your fucking phone? Ohh, you've got company, sorry! Damn! What?! Mercedes, Is that you?"

Shock is all over my face as well. "Lorenzo, Hey there!"

"Man, Lo, I am taking my key back if you do not stop

using it!" Alex says.

"Whatever! Never mind that! Mercedes how are you? What are you doing here? Where are the kids? I thought that was your truck outside!" Lorenzo is clearly tickled about what he walked into. He leans in to kiss my cheek.

"Uh, Alex and I are just talking, and we went for a swim. The kids are not here."

"So how have you been, Mercedes? It has been, what, a couple of years?"

"Hey, you left me in the car. Is he ok? You know how he was when he and Mer- Oh! Mercedes! Hi!" Lozanda, Lorenzo's wife walks in. Lozanda, the Cuban storm of clichés, everything you think of when you think of a Latina, that is Lolo. She is a very educated woman, but you would not know it when she is speaking casually. She is a real estate attorney, and she is a totally different character when she is wearing her lawyer's cap. She is curvy and petite. I am 5'7" and I am nearly 1 whole foot taller than her, but she makes up the difference with wearing the highest heels possible. And Lil Lolo loves the weave; she always wears her hair in these Godiva lengths, long super wavy and curly, and she is not afraid to experiment with color. Today it is jet black and is pulled back from her face with a sparkly headband that looks almost like a tiara. She is wearing a baby doll t-shirt with the Lion King on it, and the tightest Capri jeans I have ever seen on anyone. I look down and I see, of course, leopard print C. Louboutin's platform, peep-toe stilettos. I look at what I am wearing, and I am becoming painfully more aware that I am naked under this robe and this very private moment has way too many guests. Lozanda air kisses each of my cheeks. "I do not want you to get this red lipstick on your pretty face, honey, you are glowing! What are you doing here?" She nudges Lorenzo in the shoulder. "We just came over to check on Alex. I was telling Lorenzo that he was probably ok. I had no idea he was doing REALLY GREAT!" She winks at me when she notices our being in robes, and our clothes are littered across the lanai. "I told you, Lo, Alex did not sound depressed on the message he left." She turns to me, "You know, Mercedes, Alex and Raemier are divorced now, huh? Did he tell you? He divorced that awful cow."

"Uh, yes, he told me, Lozanda." Don't hold back, Lolo! What did you call me when we got divorced?

"Yes, Lozanda, Mercedes came, uh-er, to help me

celebrate."

"Well…" I begin to say.

"She came too?" Lorenzo says and he begins to crack up. His pun was not lost on any of us.

Alex clears his throat, "Alright Lo and Lolo, since you can clearly see that I am in good hands, Beautiful hands." He smiles at me. "I am not at ALL depressed or disappointed about my second divorce. I will ask you both to take your leave, so that I may return to my company and finish celebrating the freedom I now have. I love you and your concern for me, but you both have to go!" Alex puts his arms around each of their shoulders and he begins to walk them both back inside the house. Lorenzo, on his way back inside grabs a few pieces of fruit and bread as he makes his way past the table. "Alright, Alex, bye Mercedes, it was great to see you again." He elevates his voice over his shoulder as Alex pushes him and his wife through the house to the front door, "I hope to see you and the kids really soon now that our family is back together again!"

I get up to watch as Alex hugs them both and shuts the front door behind them.

"You have impeccable timing, Mr. Sterling." I say to him when he returns.

"How so?"

"The robes. If they came in 20 minutes earlier, I am sure they would have seen us naked."

We both start laughing. "True!" he says, and we laugh even harder. "Well, sweetheart, I think our secret will be out soon. You know that neither Lozanda nor Lorenzo can keep anything to themselves, especially if it is someone else's business. And, for it to have been you sitting here with me, anyone else would not have been so sensational to them."

"Would there have been anyone else?"

"No, not for me."

"Good answer, Mr. Sterling, good answer!"

"I say that we have maybe 30 minutes before everyone knows that we are back together."

I cough and pretend that it was the bread I had just placed in my mouth, but, does he think that we are back together? Just like that? No way. I still am not sure.

CHAPTER 3

"Hell no, she is not going to win! I worked too hard to get the life I deserve, and what does he think? Is he just going to give it all back to her? Does he think that I am going to just let him? Hell fucking nah!"

Raemier is talking to herself as she runs back to her SUV that is parked down the street from the house she and Alexander used to share. She pulls off her wig, throws it on the passenger seat. She is furious after she watched through the fence as Alex and Mercedes in the pool fooling around. She is shaking as she remembers their embracing and intimate whispering to each other. She recalls the way Alexander was looking at that homewrecking bitch. The longing look in his eyes, he never had for her. They never had that kind of intimacy! Why does she get everything?! How is that he is capable of being everything for his Mercedes, and not even half of that for her? She is breathing heavily, and she can barely hold and turn the keys in the ignition. The car starts and it startles her as if she was not the one turning the key. Raemier tries to calm herself so that she can drive to her temporary residence at her sister's house. Even the thought of that makes her rage even more. That bitch got a huge house after she divorced that bastard and I have NOTHING! Damn prenupt! He has to pay for what he has done to me! This is not where I disappear into the background and he can just tidy up his life with her and sweep me under the rug! Damn that! Bitch-assed mother fucker must be crazy! He will pay!

The following weeks were filled with more "courting" from Alexander Sterling. Intimate dinner dates. I received flowers every other day. Sometimes he sends two or three bouquets after a special night together. Alex has been sending me flowers for each time we loved, creating a small botanical garden in my wing of the house. It is beautiful to see, but sometimes, I think that it is him trying to push "us" out into the open. I know he senses my hesitation to tell everyone about "us". I am still not sure. We were both very surprised that Lorenzo and Lozanda were discrete and kept our relationship between the four of us. I would even add that I was relieved. I convinced Alex to keep our relationship between us. The roses and various flower arrangements I have been receiving are all beautiful. Before now, I cannot recall him ever making me feel this special. I feel regal and cherished by this attention, but the more I receive, the more I believe they are just Alex screaming "Tell them about us!" The attention also makes me fearful. Fearful, this all is not completely real. Fearful that if I concede, Alex could or would change his mind once he feels the challenge of getting me back has been met; or, fearful that I will be the one changing my mind. The kids think that their dad is trying to woo me back, and being wooed by anyone is fine with me. Especially being wooed by Alex because it vindicates my ego. Let the boys see how to win someone back, but hopefully they will never hurt anyone and have to woo them back. But, who are we kidding, these are Alex's boys. His spitting images and his confidence and both have tons of it for a lifetime. I only hope that the good parts of both of us are in all of them, deep and strong. Alex only asks that I "try" at getting us together, so here I am "trying," and I am having a great time at it, too. It's just that sometimes it feels like I am trying to swim freely, but, not really, because I still have one hand gripping the wall.

Alexis informed my parents of her daddy's intentions of winning us back and of his second divorce being filed. My mom called and ranted at me for over an hour before my dad made her stop. He reminded my mom that I am an adult and therefore capable of making my own decisions. So, I was glad when my father took the phone from her and said that he "was fine with whatever decision I made for my family." Mother, my maternal grandmother, said that I should consider reconciling with Alex, because in her opinion, men make mistakes. She felt they should not be punished when they finally grow up and realize that they made one or more major mistakes and then want to make up for it. Furthermore, since, I had not moved on, why not?

He is the father of my children. Mother, she is so old-school. My mom, on the other hand, not so much. Lately, she has made it her mission to constantly remind me of how devastated I was when we were together before and how unmatched we are for each other. How much he has hurt me and the children. Even, before leaving to be with Raemier, Alex never really appreciated me, she says, and so on and so on. I suppose, I am to relive every painful memory, replaying every transgression we heaped on each other. Every pain Alex caused her daughter and thus pains for her. She pulled out everyone she knew of and laid it on the table for me to see. Now, she is being passive aggressive and has limited her conversations with me. I guess it is because my dad put his foot down, and now she feels we do not have much to say to each other. She does not want to hear anything about Alexander and how happy I am with him, outside of "Hello, Good-bye, and I love you's."

This evening Alexis and Alex are having their annual Father/Daughter Dance with our social club, Diamonds of Excellence. This year, she wants a more "grown up" dress, no more little girl dresses, and she has been dragging me from store to store, mall to mall, looking for that special and perfect dress. The dress she has in her head, the one that does not seem to exist in the real world, or at least in the city of Tampa.

"Alexis, we need to hurry up and pick a dress." I am exasperated, as I am holding up three dresses I would love for her to pick from. Not only are they not THE DRESS, but her little face is screwed up so much at the sight of them that you would have thought I was holding up dirty diapers for her to inspect. "Remember, once we find the dress, we still have to accessorize and it is almost noon!" I have not told her yet, but her father and I have bought her, her first diamond jewelry. We have already picked out a matching tiny drop earring and pendant set, three-stone princess cut diamonds, and each stone graduated in size. I am anxious to get to the jeweler on the other side of the mall to pick up the package so I can see her face when she opens it.

"I know, mama!" She looks past me and exclaims, "Ohhh! Hi Desiree! Mama look, it is Desiree!"

I turn to see her friend, the ever-stylish Desiree and her dad Stephen. They are apparently last minute shopping for tonight's event, like we are. Stephen is laden with shopping bags. His face looks happy, but tired, like his wallet more than likely. Although, painful, shopping for fashion is one thing his wife, Denere, and daughter can do quickly. I know from experience. By the looks of some of the bags, they are not all for Desiree, so Denere must be somewhere nearby.

"Hi, Mercedes how is shopping going?" he asks me.

"Hello, Stephen, apparently not as well as Denere and Desiree! Where is Denere, anyway?"

"Here I am! How are you Mercedes?" Denere is walking up to us as she has her cell phone up to her ear. She kisses my cheek, "Lady, what have you been up to?"

I give her a quick hug, "Nothing much just our last minute looking for Alexis' dress."

"Umm hmm!" She winks at me. "That is not what I heard." She then returns to her phone conversation. "You did WHAT?! No!" She walks off in another direction to continue her phone conversation.

I look at Stephen.

He smiles and shrugs, "Work. She is planning the fall fashion show."

He and I stand back in silence and watch our girls browse through several racks of semi-formal dresses.

"So, Stephen, what has Desiree picked to wear tonight?" I ask.

"Some glittery, silky dress that is way too grown up for our 11-year-old daughter. I was outvoted, but what can I do? I am an old fuddy-duddy dad who 'knows nothing about fashion'! As long as everything is covered up, I am grateful."

Stephen used to be a "confirmed" bachelor, until his late 40's until the handsome neurosurgeon met and fell hard for his beautiful and exotic six-foot Sudanese super-model wife Denere. Denere, fifteen years his junior, is more than super-model beautiful. She is intimidatingly beautiful and as beautiful on the inside as well. She hit the jackpot when she met and fell in love with the handsome Dr. Whitmore, one of the Southeast's top ten premier neurosurgeons and number thirty-seven in the world. Denere having retired from the world of modeling has opened her own chain of high-end boutiques and three health and wellness clubs called "Jet." If you ask her, she is now far more domesticated than she could have ever imagined and she loves every minute of it.

Worldwide jet-setting was their thing when it was just the two of them. They would travel to small countries, barely blips on the globe, for his yearly "Doctors Without Borders" philanthropy program and she would take him with her to photo-shoots in the most amazing locations. That was all before she became pregnant with the triplets, but one thing has not changed, they were inseparable then and even more so now. Desiree and her two brothers, Seven and Stephan, have slowed down the jet-setting, but they still manage to see the world together. I am still waiting for her to slow down enough so that we can catch up on their latest travels. She loves and adores her husband, and he loves and adores her. Their family is solid and strong, and that is what I am looking for and wanting for our family, God willing. They will always be mindful of what they have together, take care of each other and not blow it.

"Mommy, mommy! How about this one?" I turn, from my mental musings, to see my darling princess holding up a way too sexy, slinky rhinestone and sequined halter dress she found with Desiree's help. Something that would look great in my closet! (If I were 30 pounds lighter and 10 years younger, that is!) I sigh and glance at Stephen who is amused, and he chuckles and shrugs his shoulders at me.

"She has obviously forgotten that she is my daughter, and that she is only 11 years old! Why do-little girls want to grow up so fast?" I say to him. I then turn to my waiting puppy-eyed princess and say the word she has been dreading that I would say to her, "NO!"

"Aww! Mommy!"

I turn back to Stephen and say, "Here we go again! I will see you all later! Tell Denere to call me later. Alexis, please tell Dr. Whitmore and Desiree goodbye."

"Good-bye Dr. W, good-bye D! Come on, mommy! Please! This is THE Dress! It is beautiful! Look how it sparkles and as we always say, 'you can never have too much sparkle!"

"Good-bye Mercedes and I will see you later tonight, Alexis." Stephen tells us.

I shake my head no and I take the sparkling prize from her hands and hang it back up. We are back at square one and time is fleeting. Wow, procrastination really sucks! My cell phone rings. It is Alex's personal ringtone, Beyonce's Upgrade You. Butterflies take flight…

"Hey!"

"Hello. Are you having any luck yet with the shopping?"

The butterflies turn to doves when I hear his voice. Large, full-grown doves flying freely within me. Yeah, he does this to me.

"No, no luck at all. We aren't finding anything age appropriate for the tween-ager. You would think that after searching three of Tampa's largest malls and several other boutiques in Hyde Park and South Tampa, we would have found something by now. I now know what I should be when I grow up, a tween fashion designer."

"You should. You have always been a great artist, and you have a great eye for clothes. Hey, don't you have a friend in fashion, too?"

"Yes, I do. Dr. Stephen Whitmore's wife Denere. That is funny that you mentioned her, we just bumped into them here at the mall."

"See I forgot, she was the one married to Stephen. You should look into doing that for real. Seriously, Mercey. I will look into financial projections and give you a feasibility spreadsheet for start-up costs. Hmmmm. Yes, interesting. I never considered that for you. That is something I can put together for you in a day or two. You know, just so that you can have a prospectus, you know, what to expect for that path."

His mind has begun calculating and I think that I have lost him to numbers and financial projections.

I have always been his project since I dropped out of college almost 20 years ago. I think that his guilt has him constantly wanting to help me, in any way he can, trying to figure out the different ventures for me to repair the life I should have had before he destroyed it. If I can find me, then I can agree to our being a "we" again, I suppose. When I went back to school this year, he paid for my tuition and books. He is always trying to make up for our past. I like it, but it is hard to be grateful when I feel that he owes me this and much more. I know that if we are to continue in this relationship, I must let him off the hook for the past. I am (we are) a work in progress.

I decide to interrupt his mechanical mind, free him from trying to plan my immediate future and bring him back to the present. "Maybe I will think about that as a possible plan for my future, but that will not help us for tonight. So, what is up with you?"

"Nothing, I just wanted to hear your voice."

"Really? My stressed-out voice will help you, how?"

We laugh.

"Well, I did not expect you to be stressed out, too."

"Too? Why, is there something wrong?"

"Yes. No. Well, yes but …. Nothing for you to worry about."

"Well, if this relationship, we are trying to have, is going to move into something more permanent, then we must communicate better."

"True, but I do not want to lay this on our fragile and young new relationship already. At least not yet"

"Wow, is it that bad? You are scaring me."

"I do not want you to worry about this, especially today. Today is supposed to be a special night for the princess and me, and I am looking forward to our date tonight. Reggie and I are taking the girls to dinner before the dance, you know, to show them how a man is supposed to behave when courting a young lady. Reggie said we are going to set a precedent - a standard."

"I like that." I am smiling, and then I frown. Did he just do a Jedi-mind trick and change the subject on me? Oh no he didn't! "Nice try, Alex, what is going on?"

"Oh, you caught that switch out, did you?"

"Yes, spill it."

"Alright" he sighs, then takes another deep breath "Raemier called me earlier and said that Adrian and Andre were just arrested for fighting at their neighborhood park. Adrian was talking to a girl who was there watching them play basketball. Evidently, she had a boyfriend whom she thought she had broken up with, who saw them and came after Adrian with a baseball bat. Adrian was able to dodge the bat. He and Andre threw a few punches and then Andre pulls out a gun and shoots it up in the air when the other kid's friends start to join in. The fight is stopped just shy of broken bones and teeth. But, there was a police officer in the area and heard the gunshot and he arrested the boys." He purges this information in record speed, and I doubt that he breathed since he began telling me what has happened. I, myself, am hardly breathing when I finally respond to what he just told me.

"Are you serious?! Ehrr, where would he get a gun from? He is only 13 for goodness sake!"

"Yes. I have no idea. I looked in my gun locker and all of mine are accounted for. I have no idea. Lorenzo said that it was 9mm and he is not telling us where he got it. They are both being held for that reason. They are playing the twin switch-er-oo trying to pretend that they both had the gun so neither will be the only one getting in trouble. I have my suspicions of who gave it to them, Raemier's family is hood, you know."

"I did not know that." I, of course, suspected it, but I never knew it for sure. Oh, by the way, if you are curious, this news shot my stomach doves right between their eyes. Dead. I could cough up feathers. Really.

"She is from the hood, and she is one of 10 kids, and several of them are firmly planted on the 'wrong side of the tracks'. I suspect an uncle, a cousin, maybe even an aunt to be a supplier, not cool. When I find out whom, which one of these dumb asses did give him the gun; I am going to fuck them up."

Ignoring that last comment, I ask "What are you going to do about the boys?"

"Let them sit until Monday. Let them learn that there are consequences for their actions. You know, they have to take responsibility for stupid decisions. Things that my parents were really light on teaching me and my siblings. You know they always bailed us out."

"But today is Saturday!" I say. I would hate if it were

one of my boys. I believe in tough love, but this gun thing is serious.

"I know, but Mercey, they are not cooperating, and they do not understand the gravity of their situation. I will help them out when they start helping themselves out. They have the nerve to tell the officers there that they are not 'snitches'. I am going to let them sweat this out."

"But, Alex, what if they lose their trust in you?"

"They need to learn, Mercey, and if I do not teach them, this world will eat them alive. They have no idea where these choices they are making will lead them. They need to see that whomever gave them the gun is sitting back and watching them suffer for it. They aren't stepping up to help them. Raemier, of course, does not like the decision, she also says that if this were Aren and Avery, I would not be doing this to them. She is wrong you know. I would."

For a second, I have to think how I would really feel about this. If Aren or Avery had a gun, how would I have handled it? I would want them to learn their lesson, and I am not a stranger to tough love with my children. Yeah, I must admit, I would let them sweat it out too if they were not cooperating with the authorities or their parents and uncle. "Hell, I would too, I guess. I just pray that they would never put us to the test."

"Yeah, pray. Mercey, they are all good kids, but I have to admit that I am not surprised by the twin's behavior. Their environment is different around their mother's family. Even if her mother is a damn good psychiatrist, they just have a lot of bad seeds. The twins just lack the confidence that Aren and Avery have naturally. Adrian and Andre are in constant competion with each other, their brothers, school mates, shit, everyone. It is, as if, they have to prove something to everyone. Why? I have no idea!"

"You are right, Aren and Avery are even- tempered and they have had very few issues with confidence. It comes from us letting them know that whenever they screw up, they can depend on us to help them through it."

"Yes, help them, not rescue them."

"Yeah, but do not forget when they were 'acting the fool' four years ago."

He chuckles, "Yeah, but even then, they knew their

limits, and not to over-step them. It was growing pains, and they were confused about our divorce and me leaving our family for Raemier. It was clear to them, I was not happy there. They could see us fighting all the time and it confused them."

"Wait, you guys have been arguing back then?"

"Are you kidding? We argued all the fucking time. We argued over our kids, yours and mine, over our own twins, over the moon, the sky and stars! She said that I preferred our children over the twins. This was especially her favorite argument when our children came over to my house to stay."

"Really, I had no idea." I really had no clue. It saddens me that my kids did not have a safe haven at any of our homes. In our home, they had a mother who would not come out of her room for days, letting my mom, grandmother and their nanny take care of the important things like feeding them and caring for them. Now, I see that their stepmother resented their time with their father. They had an evil stepmother. They never complained, never. People have always asked me why my kids were so close with each other.

Now I can see why and how it happened. They rarely fight or bicker with each other. I feel the angry mother bear in me rise up, let me find out she harmed my babies! The angry bear turns and looks at me angrily and says in my voice, "bitch you hurt them too!", she stretches and lies back down with a huff. She is right, Raemier was steamrolling them at their dad's house and I was in a black hole at home. I watch Alexis as she walks ahead of me. I decide that I need to hear from my own daughter exactly how Raemier treated them. Damn Alex for bringing this rabid bitch into our lives!

"Mercey, did I lose you?"

"Alex!" I forgot that we were still on the phone. "Yes, I was thinking about how I cannot stand you for bringing this bitch into our lives."

"Yeah, I am sorry for that."

"Yeah, well, sorry is … well, it is sorry. Alex, let me call you back."

"Sure. We have to talk about this."

"Yeah, I know, but while we have been talking, Alexis still needs a dress and I have to go to the jewelers still. And she has a date with a very special man in her life."

"Oh! I am only special to her?"

"Ha! Seriously, I am sorry to hear about the boys. I hope that they come out of this better for it. Is Lo going to help them?"

"Yes, Lo, the attorney extraordinaire is on the j-o-b. We have already gone down there and talked with them. As far as they know, they will be there, in "jail," for a while. They are not to talk to anyone unless their uncle is present. Do you know the police tried to interrogate them - minors! Lo was mad as hell when he got there and saw them talking to the twins. There will be some jobs lost after my brother is through with all of this."

"Wow, that is out of pocket, they should not have done that. Ok, Alex, I have to go." As I watch Alexis pop into yet another store still in search of this elusive dress. "I am sorry to hear about the twins. I know that Lorenzo will take care of them. They are in good hands with the two of you handling things. I will definitely pray about this situation. They are good kids, just a little misguided. I am glad that you confided in me. No secrets. I will call you after we leave the mall. Bye." I rush my sentences to him, wanting to distance myself from this mess and hurry up and end this manic search for this dress.

"Alright then goodbye, Mercey, I love you."

I pause, wait ….. What did he just say? Does he think that we are at "that PLACE" yet?

"Did you hear me Mercey? I said I love you."

Uhh "Uhh, thanks? (cough) I am not ready for this declaration yet." I whisper.

"Oh. Ok. I know one day soon you will be. I hope." He chuckles but I hear the nervous uncertainty in his voice. This is new, hardly is he ever uncertain. Even superman has his kryptonite, have we found his?

"I guess. You do know that I do care for you? I will always care for you. I am just not ready for being in love with you again."

"I know that you think that I will "demolish" us again. I can wait until you are ready."

"I do believe that you will not intentionally want to."

"Ok. I will let you go. Call me later?"

"I will. What time do you want Alexis ready?"

"By 6"

"Ok. Later then."

"Yeah, later"

He hangs up. I know that I disappointed him, but what should I have done? What could I say? I would be lying to myself and to him if I had said that I loved him. I do not feel love. I feel lust, familiarity, comfort, but I honestly do not feel love! Whatever that is, so, oh well. Oh, and this time if I say it, to him or to anyone, I really want to mean it! Lord knows what we had before could not have been real love, or was it? Well, no he was too selfish, I was too dumb, and we both were dysfunctional.

With that I look at my watch and gasp. Ughhh!! Where had the time gone? At this point, I just want to go home and pick any one of the Disney Princess costumes she has in her closet! I take Alexis into the juniors' department at a nearby department store and we finally compromise on a sparkly, rhinestone dazzler that covers my child up and satisfies her "fashion jollies" from it as well. Sad thing is, we started off in this very same store, but somehow, we missed this or maybe we did see it and it was 'no' either by me or her. Whatever the case may be, it is a resounding 'yes' right now, and I am hungry! We make a quick stop to the jeweler, and I manage to get a quick glance at our newly boxed contents while she is mesmerized by all the diamonds in their display cases. She is definitely my child. She is going to love this! I am a little disappointed that I cannot give it to her right now, but I did promise Alex to wait until we were together. He wants to see her face light up, too. I cannot blame him, Alexis is a ray of light. I smile at her and take her hand and say, "Let's go find something to eat!"

We settle at a Chinese fast-food counter and order Lo mein and sweet and sour chicken. We find a table in the busy food court and sit our food and packages down. I decided I will pick my princess' brain about Raemier. I have barely had time to sit down when I noticed that Alexis has begun shoveling her food in her mouth. Whoa! We must have a few etiquette classes soon, real soon! Coming from the old guard, I am surprised that my mom or even Mother have not said anything to me by now about Alexis' manners. My children should have already had their etiquette classes by now. I will look this week to make sure the 3 of them get into Ms. Esmeralda's School of Etiquette. Maybe, I will even include the twins. Whoa! Am I making family plans including the twins? I really must figure out what it is I want to do with all of this. I look back at what was once my sweet little angel and how she has been replaced by a cute but piggy-girl. This is really alarming; what I am watching here? When did she pick up such bad habits? Did she just slurp? I even swear, I just heard her snort! I just heard my daughter snort and slurp her food! Now add a gulp of her green tea and she is back to smacking and chewing with her mouth wide open!

"Alexis!"

"Huh?"

"Huh?"

"Sorry, yes ma'am?"

"First of all, did you even say your grace? And secondly, since when do we eat like pigs at the trough?"

"Oh, I am sorry mommy. I am hungry! Shopping takes a lot out of me!"

"So much so that you forget your home training? Come on now!"

She grins sheepishly at me, and she closes her eyes and begins to move her lips silently in prayer. All the while her fork is poised hovering over her plate in mid-air and loaded with her next bite to be eaten. I laugh at the spectacle that is my baby girl.

"Amen." The fork goes into her mouth more reserved, and she chews like I have always taught her, as if the previous display never happened. It is so nice to see that she has not completely lost it. I let her take a few more bites before I decided to begin my inquisition. I do not know why I would want to disrupt our pleasant day by bringing up this bitch-heifer, but these are things I should and need to know. I am disappointed with myself for not inquiring earlier; but I have been in such a fog for the last few years, that I took a lot for granted.

"Alexis?" I begin.

"Yes, mommy?"

"I would like to ask you some questions about your time over your father's house. Has Raemier, Adrian, or Andre ever hurt you or your brothers? You know, has Raemier ever been mean or has she said mean things to you or about you or your brothers?"

"No, mommy, she is very nice to us, and my brothers, I love them! I love them all. Andre can be moody and when he acts like that, we just leave him alone. He yelled at his mom and at daddy once, but he stopped when I started to cry. Avery took him outside to talk and he was happy again when they came back inside. But, we all take care of each other. You know, Raemier was mean to daddy, though."

"Really, how so?"

"You know."

"No, I do not. Tell me."

"Well… they would go into their bedroom and argue a lot."

"What were they arguing about, do you know?"

"No, I am not sure exactly, but I do remember her saying that daddy did not really love her."

"Did you hear her reason for saying that?"

"I do not know, but I do not think he loved her either."

"Why?" I swallow hard. I cannot imagine what my 11-year-old would know about love.

"Well." I watch her chew her food and it appears to me is that she is choosing her next words. "He never smiles when he talks to her. You know how he does when he talks to us, the twins, and…. when he talks to you. I can't explain it."

Yes, you can sweetheart, you just explained it very well.

I nod my head and say, "I understand exactly what you mean, darling, exactly what you mean." I smile at her.

Then just like that she dives back into her food. I tasted mine for the first time, and I see exactly why she was eating so ravenously moments ago. Apparently, I am "starving" too! We eat our food and chit-chat about the nonsense that fills in the spaces in our life. We are carefree, light, and airy all at once. I let go of the mama bear rage I want to punish Raemier with, I give in to the moment. This moment I am in, here with one of the loves of my life, and there is noone insignificant here, like Raemier, in this moment. I see Raemier as someone who has missed out on something so vital all the while she was chasing after her conquest of "winning " Alex. She forgot to make sure whether he was, in fac, the one she really wanted, and whether he was capable of being what she needed. I empathize with her briefly but let her leave my mind. She's lost and misguided too; like her boys, and, if I can admit it, like me at times.

As we resume our shopping for shoes and hair accessories, I cannot help but feel anxiety about where my life is heading. My mind is racing. How can I get back with Alex? With our history and now a little glimpse of our future with an additional two teenagers thrown into the mix, I MUST BE CRAZY! I look at the time displayed on the giant clock in the middle of the mall, it is already 2:15. I have to get Alexis to her 3 o'clock hair appointment to get her hair blown straight for tonight. Why on earth does she wants to straighten her long dark brown curly crown is downright absurd; but, I allow this "treat" once a quarter. She will be in our pool ruining it by tomorrow anyway. I tell her that we must leave now, because, Mrs. Isabella does not "do" late appointments and we are at least 20 minutes away. We rush to the valet and depart to Mrs. Isabella's Salon. We arrive at the South Tampa Salon in record time, no speeding of course. I order up mani/pedis for the princess and I and we begin our beauty preparations for the evening. The King's chariot arrives at 6, and we will be there waiting with cute fingers and toes.

"Mama?"

"Yes?"

"Can I get tips put on, with a few rhinestones?"

"No tips, Lexi!! But you can get a couple of stones."

"Awwww mommy, I need tips!!! Please?!?!"

Here we go again!

CHAPTER 4

"You did not call me back." I hear hurt in his voice when I see him standing in my doorway.

I took him in, looking delicious in a tuxedo! His height and mass, tucked exquisitely in a wool/silk suit is any woman's wet dream. Even his smell is intoxicating.

"I know, I am sorry." I kiss his cheek and let him in the house. "Your daughter is a handful when shopping. How is everything with the twins?"

He sighs heavily, "There has been no change. They have both stopped talking, even to their uncle. They are scared and to be honest, so am I a little bit now.

Andre and Adrian have tattoos. I had no idea. Some kind of tribal symbols. I have no clue when they got them but there are several different parts of their bodies covered usually by clothes, on their arms, shoulders, and their back."

I gasp, "no way!"

"Yes and I do not know what they mean, either; whether they are gang related or just youthful rebellion. They are 13 for God's sake. Who do they know that would tattoo kids?"

We stand in the foyer shaking our heads and looking at the floor. I look up into Alex's face and there is such raw concern for his children written all over it. The angst pools in his eyes, he is drowning, and I have no way to save him. I say another silent prayer for this situation, and a prayer for direction and discernment. There must be a way. Your children become your world the minute they are born. It is so hard to see them make such huge mistakes with their own lives. Especially when, like Alex and myself, shit like most parents, we are still making our own life mistakes.

I give him a quick hug and break the silence. "Come, let's go into the kitchen. I was cooking dinner for me and the fellas." I take his hand and lead him to the heart of my castle. "Are you sure that you are up for tonight? Alexis, will be ok, you know, she will understand. They are her brothers, and she loves them so much."

He chuckles and I see a spark in his eyes. "No way in hell would I miss this date with Lexi. She would have my neck if I broke our plans. No thank you! I will not break a date with my princess nor my queen, ever." He winks and lifts my hand and kisses it. He spins me around and he kisses me lightly. It was a defibrillator, the electricity shocking awake those dead doves in my stomach. I feel them stirring. He kisses me again, deeper this time. Clear! The doves are stirring a little more, trying to take flight. The third kiss was his naturally greedy kiss - the one that makes this girl's panties hit the floor. I feel myself gasping and breathing deeply at the same time. I love the awakening he is giving my body. My senses are overloaded with his cologne and his natural scent. He pulls away just before I lose myself completely. I feel the limpness fade away and I notice that I was being fully supported upright by Alex's embrace. Yes, honey, all wrapped up in his fit and fabulous arms. He places me on my feet again, but he is still holding me.

"Are you alright?" he asks me throatily.

"uhhhh mmmm yessss." I purred. Yes, that is right, I purred my Eartha Kitt, cat-woman, All of that! Oh, my Gemini gremlin meant all of that! I do not subscribe to the horoscope, zodiac nonsense, but, I do know that more times than not, I am susceptible to Gemini ways. I do not understand it, so I will not try to explain it; but, most times, I find myself fitting the description of the cosmic sign I was born under. Sometimes, I am double minded, especially when it comes to me and Mr. Alexander Sterling. "Torn" seems to be my constant state. I find my normal voice and say finally, "Let me go upstairs and check on Alexis. Please check on the quiche in the oven for me when the timer goes off. There is some iced tea on the island if you are thirsty. You know where everything is."

I turn from him, and he playfully smacks my behind. "Hurry up!" he says. There was way too much jiggle for my pleasure, but I giggled a satisfactory response for his ego. I headed for the stairs, making a mental note to add more squats to my routine tonight.

I make my way up the grand staircase to the children's wing of the house. When we built this house, there was nothing I could ask for that Alex would not have given to me. I asked for it and he gave it to me. I was just pregnant with Aren, and it must have been his guilt at the time. I thought that he was being a "good husband." He was just trying to be the calm before a storm called Raemier. I had no idea what was to come in a short spance of a few months. Thinking back about then, this house probably made Raemier go even more over the edge. She wanted me to know that my "perfect life" was not real. She had to shatter what she saw as my "picture perfect life." When my husband was in her bed with her. Probably making similar promises to her, but his promises to me were actually being carried out. That would make anyone fighting mad.

She was shouting "Hey Bitch! Fuck You! I am here! I exist and I got your man between my legs!!" She took advantage of the power Alex gave her. Will I be letting the madness continue if we get back together completely? Will she be pulling Alex's strings and continue to make my life hell? With her, it is what it is. She is "coo-coo for cocoa puffs" for real! Has he really exorcized her influence in his life? I really never understood their, his, attraction in any way. What about her made him want to risk losing his family anyway? What about their relationship made him reckless with ours? We were already married and had Avery. What was it about her? What was she giving him that I was not, or that he felt that I could not give him? What I know for sure is that when we moved into this huge home, we were no longer the family I thought we were; especially, when we began its construction. Now, we have this huge "dream" home; and, if I am not careful, I will be the only one left in it to enjoy it. In 7 short years, Alexis will graduate from High school and will leave me here all alone.

The configuration of all seven bedrooms is the same. Of course, my master being twice as big, and it is in its own wing. In the boys' rooms there are differing themes. Avery has the planets of the solar system on the walls and antique arcade video games plus a large work island for his science experiments and robotics in his lounge area. Aren has music notes and recording artists' posters, and lyrics to songs for his room's theme, real usable instruments are hung up delicately on his walls next to a sound room and studio recording equipment. There are fiber-optic "stars" on all their ceilings. For Alexis there are princes, princesses, fairies, dragonflies, butterflies, unicorns, castles, and fireflies all over her walls. Some of them glow in the dark adding more whimsy and fantasy to her suite's four chambers. I enter Alexis's lounge to her huge bedroom suite. In her bedchamber there is a large queen bed, ornately decorated with crystals, rhinestones, and glitter ("you can never have too much sparkle" is our motto), with 4 thick posts a pink, purple and orange linen, and chiffon draped canopy on a raised half foot platform with a golden crown and tulle framing the head of the bed. There is a matching writing desk and another sitting area next to a matching bookcase. I want my daughter to be cocooned in fantasy for as long as she can stand it. She has her whole life to live in reality. If I can provide her with a little "magical" place that is her own, who cares? I know, you may think that we take the whole royalty, king/queen, and princes/princess theme too far with my family, but I think that I am really too sedate with it. I could really amp it up more, but I keep it in check so others will not think that I am "too far gone." Plus, my decorator cut me off; I think Alex had something to do with it, because she was all for it at first then suddenly, she shut it down. Bling it up and bling it out, the more the merrier! I have found a few treasures that I have added. Not tacky, though. The kids often tell me when I am going overboard. But any-who, I love it! So does Alexis (It is thanks to my influence all of these years, I know!).

Further into her suite, before you get to her walk-in closet and ensuite bathroom with garden tub and separate shower and custom vanity with sink, there in her dressing room is where I find her, standing before her three paneled full-length dressing mirrors. She is making her dress twirl, and she spins around admiring all angles of her new ensemble. Her freshly straightened hair is pushed back off her face with her new tiara-like headband, freely moving as she dances. I lean on the door frame to the dressing room and watch the Alexis "show." She is really feeling her look for the night.

"Look at her dance! Beauty incarnate." I feel Alex walk up behind me and he places his arms around my shoulders. He whispers into my ear, "I missed you and you were taking too long. The quiche is fine, and I took it out" he plants a small kiss on my temple, and smiles.

"Daddy!" She runs over to us. "You are right on time!" She stops in front of us and twirls herself again.

Alex beams at her, "You are as beautiful as ever! Just like your mommy. Are you ready for our evening of dinner and dancing? Your chariot awaits!"

I am gushing looking at the two of them.

"Oh daddy, you are so pretty in your suit!"

"It is a tux, Lexi and daddy is handsome not pretty. Pretty is for girls." Aren says as he enters into Alexis' room. "Hey dad!"

"Aire! How are you? What have you been getting into?"

"I am fine. I was just writing some lyrics." Alex grabs Aren into masculine embrace and he kisses the top of his head. By the looks of it, the 6'3" dad will not be able to do that too much longer. My babies are growing up so fast. I think of their births and now images rush in of girls, guns, and gangs and all too quickly the moment is ruined, thanks to my over-active brain.

"Where is Avery, is he here?" Alex asks.

"Nah, he drove down to Brianna's. Something about helping her dad change the oil on her car." Aren says.

"Hey! I am supposed to be teaching him how to do that!"

"Wait a minute, Mr. Maserati and Range Rover, do you even know how to do any of that?" I ask.

"Yes I do, thank you very much! I had to with my previous cars when I was younger. You remember those cars?" He leans in to kiss me quickly. Alexis smiles and Aren makes a quick disgusted face at us, and then he smiles too." Maybe I will swing by there and see him and Dan really quick on the way out. Alright Aren, take care of mommy while your sister and I hit the town." He noogies Aren's head and he extends his elbow out for Alexis to take. We head down the stairs. "The city awaits us, so let's go!" He turns to me and winks, "I will see you afterwards."

"Eww dad, I heard that!" Aren says and quickens his steps ahead of us down the stairs.

Soon, we see lights flashing, lighting up the foyer. It is Aren and he is taking pictures of us as we descend the stairs. Avery joins him snapping pictures of his own with his camera. It is like a celebrity posing for the paparazzi. Alexis is in fits of giggles as she poses for her brothers. It is then that I remember the jewelry we bought her.

"Wait! I almost forgot!" I run to the kitchen where I hid the boxes from the jeweler. I hear Alex say, "Hey man, that was cool. You both made our day!"

"Yeah, I almost missed you guys. I am glad I didn't though." Avery is saying when I return to the foyer. Alex is hugging Avery, and he looks at me.

"Oh wow, how could I have forgotten that?" he asks.

He takes the necklace box I am offering to him, and I keep the earrings. We look at our daughter and I say, "Your father and I, have something for you."

"Yes, we have some icing to top off your look tonight."

'Icing'? I wonder how long it took for him to come up with that! We both open our boxes and Alexis and her brothers all inhale.

"What? Wait! That is for me to wear!?" Alexis squeals.

"Yes, they belong to you. You have to take care of them, do not lose them. They are real diamonds and platinum." I say.

"Yes, your mom and I think that you are ready for the responsibility of having your first diamonds." Alex says as he begins placing the necklace around her neck and he kisses her forehead.

I push back her hair and I begin affixing her new earrings.

She has a huge smile across her face. "I was wondering what earrings I was going to wear! This is awesome! Thank you!"

"Shoot, what are you two going to give us?" Avery says as he begins to take more pictures.

"I knew the day would come when Lexi would shift the balance on us for being the only girl!" Aren says with a smirk.

"Yeah, yeah, yeah!" Alex says. "You guys have season tickets to Bucs games and the Magic, and countless other things are at your disposal. And you are right, she is the only girl, so she will get a little spoiled. Just like tonight, I have to set the example that any guy she meets will have to beat what she has become accustomed to."

"That is right. So, you guys need to take notes." I chime in. "You have to treat the lady in your life to the finer things and give her the respect and love she deserves."

"And never let her forget that she is loved." He says as he looks at me. "Alright Lexi, we have to go. We cannot keep Reggie and Amber waiting."

"Here squirt you can borrow this." Avery says as he hands Alexis his treasured camera. "Take good care of it and bring it back in one piece."

"Avery, are you for real?" Alexis' eyes are large and

bright with excitement.

Alex guides our shocked daughter towards his car as she cradles the camera in her arms. She looks back at her brothers and I as we stand on the front steps waving goodbye to them, her eyes are still wide and I do think that she, for once, is speechless. Her mouth is just stuck in the huge smile she had when we placed her new jewelry on her. Alex opens the passenger door to his Maserati and helps her in the seat, he closes her door and trots to the driver's side and hops in. He waves to the three of us, as we stood there waving. We watch them as they drive down the long driveway and make their way to the gate, and as they head off down the road, on their way to a fun and fabulous time together.

"Alright guys, come on let's go eat dinner. We cannot just stand here waving like The Clampetts."

"Like who?" my boys both ask.

"The Clampetts. You know, from the Beverly Hillbillies?" I say.

They both are wearing blank stares as they look at me.

"Oh, come on! You know the Beverly Hillbillies!

The tv show?

Now we are going to watch a marathon of the Hillbillies tonight while we eat the delicious quiche I made for dinner! How is that for a Saturday night with your mom?"

CHAPTER 5

It was at 11:07 pm exactly when my world crumbled into one million tiny pieces and then those pieces were thrown into the air, taking my oxygen, and collapsing my lungs. The phone rang. That is it. A simple phone call that changed the laughter that I was sharing with my two sons as we watched DVDs of the Beverly Hillbillies. Just hours earlier, they feigned distress for having to watch an old tv show from the mid-1900s, to our really enjoying ourselves. The laughter was short lived and there were now screams, and the joy we previously felt was now replaced with pain. All because of a phone call.

The voice on the other end was my friend Dr. Stephen Whitmore, who only hours ago we had seen at the mall with his family. He told me to get to Tampa General Hospital ER immediately that Alex and Alexis were in a car accident. Stephen's voice was solemn and firm. He told me that they both were in surgery and for me to be strong. He told me that he would be there, and he would tell me more when I arrived at the hospital. I hung up the phone. I looked at my boys, put down the phone, and then I vomited.

I should have asked Avery to drive us, I now realize that I do not trust myself. I am shaking and sobbing. I was on autopilot as we flew into our garage and jumped into the truck to drive the short distance to Tampa General Hospital. The 10 minutes it took seemed like forever. All I could think was "pray Mercey" and that is what I did. I began to wonder why Stephen was the one who called me, wasn't he at the dance too? What is going on? My inner voice is decibels above normal, and every one of my thoughts is as screams in my ears, a powder keg being shot off in my head. In the background, I hear Avery and Aren calling my family members and rallying the troops we will need to help us get through this - whatever 'this' is. Dear Jesus, please do not take my family! Not one person! PLEASE! I glance at my two young men, Aren in the rear seat texting unknown people and Avery in the passenger seat speaking to, I think, my mom from the sound of it. Both have tears rolling down their faces. We are all a shocked mess.

I screech to a halt, parking in a space way too awkwardly, but I do not care. The three of us jump out of the truck and make our way to the front of the hospital's emergency room area. As we enter and head to information, we see Denere and Stephen. Stephen in his tux and Denere in a shiny silver tracksuit, both of them running toward me, their eyes were wide with concern. Is that blood on his tux? I begin to panic. Whose blood is that?

"Stephen, what has happened? What is going on?" I scream.

"Mercedes," he leads us to some chairs in the lobby. I do not want to sit down. Denere and my sons gather around me, and Stephen sits on top of a small table in front of me. He looks tired and he takes my hands into his. He nods his head to the chair in front of him. "Please sit down." I sit, just as he asks. He looks me in the eyes, and I see the tears welling up in his deep blue eyes. He speaks, "Alex and Alexis were in a car accident after the dance."

"What? How?" I am much louder than I expected. I cannot control my voice or its volume. He isn't telling me anything! Right then, I see my parents and grandmother walking towards me. I cannot breathe. Everything is in slow motion.

Stephen continues when my parents reach us. "I have given my statement to the police at the scene."

"The scene, what scene?" alarms are ringing in my ears.

I feel his fingers on my wrists, "Mercedes, I need for you to calm down. I told you that Alex and Alexis are both in surgery and they have the best surgeons working on them right now. All we can do now is wait and pray for them. I have a nurse watching each surgery and they will come tell me, us, of the progress."

"Ok." I managed with a little more control over my voice. "So what happened?"

"She is being treated and she is in police custody." Stephen says as he looks up at Denere. I look up at her too and I see her nod for him to continue.

"Who is being treated? Who is in custody? You are not making sense to me!" I asked. I feel my mom and Mother step closer to me and my father places his hands on my shoulders.

Stephen looks at each one of us, he swallows and says, "Raemier did this. She ran into them with her SUV."

A red rage envelopes me. A black beast is awake and is alive in me. I cannot see. I am blinded with rage. All this love that is surrounding me, my family and friends, I cannot see them through the darkness that has enveloped me. I flicker in clarity when I see a nurse come to Stephen, and I notice as he leads her away from us so that he can talk in privacy. I try to focus on their faces. I am trying to see if relief passes over his face or if it is something else. I cannot see it. I am losing focus. White hot rage is coming on now. Someone tries to place their arms around me, I am trying to shake them off. Another set of arms wraps around me and the first set, stronger and more determined. I cannot shake them off and a third set, now a fourth. I am suffocating. I am drowning in a sea of negativity. All hate, and all for one person. In the recesses of my mind, I hear my father telling me to "Breathe." One word, "Breathe." His command spoken to my mind and lungs directly triggered an immediate response. My body gasped taking a first breath for what seemed like too many minutes than what is naturally allowed, and a primal moan escapes my lips. I feel strangers stirring about me, I am sure that they are all staring at me. I hear my father, mother and grandmother praying aloud. Prayers of healing, of peace and order are being offered for me and my family. My grandmother calls me out praying for peace of my chaotic mind and its desire for vengeance. She knows me, she knows me so well. I hear my sisters and brothers talking to my sons. They are probably holding them. I can hear everyone, I sense everything, but my vision is tunnelled. I want to route out Raemier's location. I want to put my mamma bear paws on her now, RIGHT NOW!

I hear Stephen's voice. It jolts me and I swing my face towards him. He holds my hands, and I feel the multiple arms embracing me loosen a little bit. I am being held like a madwoman in a straitjacket. They are not wrong. Stephen speaks again, and this time I can focus on his words.

"Mercedes?"

"Yes." I croak an overly loud but a dull, empty hollow

reply.

"That was Alex's nurse that I just spoke to. She says that he is nearly out and he is stable. He has 4 broken ribs, and some bleeding that has been closed off. He has a moderate concussion from the impact. He was thrown to the ground. You should be able to see him in recovery in about 3 hours. Do you understand?"

I nod my head and I let it drop back on whoever's forearm is under my chin. Fuck Alex. He brought her into our lives, he brought that crazy bitch. Who gives a fuck about him? "What about Alexis?" I moan.

"I am still waiting to hear from the other nurse. I will page her now if you want me to."

I lift my head to look at him and respond. Whatever my face must have looked like to him in that moment caused him to jump up and do just that. Thank you, Stephen, for not being a dumb ass right now.

"Mercedes, you need to breathe deeper than that." It was my sister Maria talking. She is ever the yogi-zen goddess, but, I do not need her shit right now. She speaks again. "Your breathing is too shallow, and you will pass out at this rate." Pass out? No, I do not want to do that. I am losing control, and that is the last thing I want to do. I need to regain control so they will let me go. I need to let them think it is ok to release me and so I can get up and find this ho and beat a hole in her ass. Hold up. My head shoots up again. Stephen said that Alex was thrown to the ground. I need to know what exactly happened.

I force myself to focus, and to put "crazy Mercey" aside for now. I whisper to whoever is nearest to me, "Please get Stephen."

My mom says, "He is right here. Just one moment. Dr. Stephen, Mercedes is asking for you."

I look up and see that he and Denere talking to another nurse nearby.

"Wait is she Alexis' nurse?" I yell.

Stephen rushes over to me, "No, no she isn't. She is a colleague of mine just asking what was happening. You know, with me standing here in a bloody tuxedo and all, she was concerned. What can I do for you? Do you need a sedative? We are still waiting for Safari to respond to my page."

Safari? Her name is Safari? Ok. Focus. "What did you mean when you said that Alex was thrown to the ground? You said that they were in a car accident and that Raemier ran into them. What exactly happened tonight?"

Before Stephen is able to respond, Denere says quickly, "Mercedes, let us just focus on prayer and sending good positive energy to Alexis and Alex right now. Let's not lose focus on what is important right now."

I ignore my friend and I look her husband in the eyes. Oh, I am focused now, really focused. I can see the dread in my friend's face. "You tell me, now, what happened to my child. What did that bitch do, Stephen? You tell me now!"

"Ok." He looks at Denere and takes a deep breath. As he continues to look at his wife, he begins talking to me, "We were all in the parking garage at the hotel. Alex had just helped Alexis into the passenger seat and was shutting the door. I saw a truck speed past me, and I grabbed Desiree and jumped out of the way in between two parked cars. I get up and I see the truck slam into Alex and his car, sending him to the wall in front of his car. The truck backs up and slams Alex's car three or four more times, I do not know exactly but it was several more times." I am holding my breath as if it was holding back the rage that was coming over me.

I heard someone gasp beside me. Stephen continues. "I could hear Alexis screaming inside. I run up to the driver's door of the truck and I see Raemier. She did not look 'right' and she was screaming at the top of her lungs. I bang on the window, and I scream at her to 'Stop' and I tell her that Alexis was in the car. She stopped screaming and looked at me, and she just stopped. Reggie and Walter pulled her out of her truck and restrained her. It was chaos. The other fathers and daughters were trying to make sense of what happened, and I rallied someone to help me check on Alexis and Alex. I worked on Alex and some other dads were trying to get Alexis out of the car. It was pretty crushed, and we had to wait until the EMTs arrived to cut her out. I think that she was trapped in the car for at least 40 minutes. I was very afraid because after a while she stopped screaming, but we were not able to get her to respond. They got her out, she was unconscious, but she had tacky rhythms and low respiration, but she was breathing. We got them both here. When I first checked on her, she had some internal bleeding and we had to stop that to know the extent of her injuries. Mercedes, you are a part of a praying family, prayer, this is all we can do right now. There is a gifted surgeon operating on her right now. You could not ask for a better surgeon than him.

I can think of no one else that I would rather have operating on me than Dr. Osbourne, really."

"Ok. Thank you for telling me. When can I see her? I know that this is a teaching hospital, and that there are surgery observation/viewing rooms. I want to go there. I need to see her. I want her to feel that I am there. That she is not alone."

"I, don't think that is a good idea. Let the doctors and nurses do what they are trained to do. It is best that they work without the added pressure of the patient's loved ones looking in. They can be free to decide what is best in that situation, at that moment. Let us give them professional courtesy. I think, no I know, that it is best to wait. I can see if Alex is far along enough for you to see him --"

"Fuck Alex!" I scream "Who gives a fuck about Alex? We would not be here if it weren't for ALEX!" Spit is flying out of my mouth as I scream more obscenities about Alex. I force myself up and I spin around to look at who is all here. I see Lorenzo, poor Lorenzo, because he looks exactly like his brother at exactly the wrong time. I charge at him, and if it were not for my father and my brother Antonio grabbing me and restraining me, and my other brother Manuel and Lozanda blocking Lorenzo, I would have scratched his eyes out. "Let me go! Let me go!" I scream and they are trying to sit me back down. I hear someone say, "I am sorry, Mercedes." I feel a pinch in my hip, and then the floor moves from under my feet. I swoon and then there is a fog. I am floating, higher and higher. I am in Fiji, swimming in my lagoon.

Chapter 6

I wake to see my sons' worried faces standing over me. I bolt upright, I can feel that I am sitting on a sofa in a darkened room. Where am I? Where is Alexis? What happened? Was it all just a nightmare? "Where am I?" I ask aloud.

I look around and I see my family, all of my family. My brothers and their wives, my sisters, and their husbands. My parents, Alex's parents. Lorenzo, Lozanda and his and Alex's sisters Sasha and her fiancé Richard, and their other sister Janeese and her husband John. Stephen and Denere are nearby where whoever injected me with whatever, had laid to sleep off its effects. No, it was not all a bad dream. This is a real, living and breathing nightmare.

Avery speaks, "We are at the hospital. They had to sedate you and we brought you in this private lounge to wait for news of Alexis."

"Yeah, mom, you really scared us for a minute there." Aren adds.

I try to smile to reassure him, but my face feels a little droopy and I still feel cloudy in my brain. "How long was I out?"

"A couple of hours." My sister Isa Mara says to me.

"Yeah, you tried to kill me!" Lorenzo says as he chuckles nervously. "One of the hazards of being a twin."

"Oh, Lorenzo! I am sorry. I do not know what came over me." I say to him. I am embarrassed. "Have we heard anything about Alexis?"

"Yes, just that she is out of surgery and she is stable." Stephen answers me.

Everyone is looking at me. My sons find spaces to sit next to me on the sofa. I hug them both and they begin to cry. I am really embarrassed now. I scared them. Instead of being a comfort for them when we are praying for their sister and their father, I gave them something else to worry about. Oh, shit! Their father! I cursed their father in my selfish rage.

"I am so sorry! I am so, so, sorry! Have you been able to go see your dad yet?"

"No. We could not leave you." Avery whispers.

"Nana, Ma'Dear and Pop-Pop went to check on him. He was still asleep." Aren adds.

"You don't. You don't really hate him, do you? You cannot blame him for this, can you mommy?" Avery asks me. He sounded so young at that moment. It is almost as if he was that tiny little boy again. The little boy whom I had to tell that his father and I were getting divorced. The little boy who cried for days because he did not understand why we were separating. Now he does not understand again how things go from sugar to shit in just a matter of hours.

What do I say to him? How can I get him to understand the underlying truths that have us sitting in the hospital waiting area while their little sister and father are fighting for their lives; and, that part of the blame can be laid firmly at their "super-father's" feet? What can I say? I look at my son's face, and all I can say is a lie.

"No, Avery, I was just very upset." Then the truth, "Raemier is responsible for her actions. She did this. Not your father."

I look at Stephen and I say, "If I cannot see Alexis now, I want to take my sons to see Alex. Please."

He nods his head, and he leads me and my sons to the door. I look back at my entire family. "I am ok now. I am sorry for the outburst earlier."

"Oh, we understand!" Mother says, and she nods me on. She knows me, she really knows me. Everyone else murmurs kind words, like "Don't worry about all that." "We know you were upset." And so on. I follow Stephen to the nurse's desk as he gets clearance for us to go in and see Alex. Lorenzo and Lozanda follow us to the desk. He hugs me and she joins in the hug. I hug them back and Lorenzo grabs the boys into our embrace. He looks at Stephen and asks, "Would it be ok if Lolo and I came too?"

Stephen nods and gets two more badges from the nurse.

The six of us walk through the double doors towards the recovery rooms where Alex is still resting, and he is waiting for a room to be moved to.

Alex's eyes are still closed when we walk into his recovery room. He must have sensed our arrival, because he weakly opens his eyes when we approach his bedside. He sighs, and he begins to cry. He whispers "Hi." He is talking to me. Directly to me. He is looking at no one else but me. I am last to enter the room, and I am now standing furthest away from him, but he sees me, only me. I cannot bring myself to move closer, I do not trust myself. To my relief Lorenzo speaks.

"Hey Alex! You look good!"

He does not break his gaze from me. "Where is Alexis?" He again whispers to me. Tears are rolling down his face.

Stephen answers for me. "She is out of surgery and in recovery. Dr. Osbourne will be out soon to tell us more."

"Good." He says. He is still looking at me, searching

my face, and I know why. He wants to know if he has lost me. I look away, I turn my back. It is too soon to let him know that he has. This is not about me; it is about these two people who need me to help them get better. They need me to be their comfort and to stand beside them through this mess. I do not know how I will be able to help Alex, especially when I cannot even look at him.

He begins to talk to Avery and Aren, then to Lorenzo and Lozanda. Stephen and I step back out into the hallway.

"You know that he did not do this, Mercedes. He was not capable of stopping this. She was not 'right' in her head. I cannot explain it, but she was 'gone.'"

"Stephen, so what, who can I blame for this? Hell, Alex isn't responsible, now Raemier isn't because she was not in her right mind? I know he did not do the actual hitting and I know Raemier is responsible for her own actions, but, at the end of the day… At the end of it all, she would not be a part of our lives if he had not involved her in our lives. Period."

"He was trying to fix that, Mercedes."

"I know. It is too late for that now." I shake my head

and I look back into Alex's room. He is looking at me, he still would not tear his gaze away from me.

They move Alex to another room, and we are still waiting for Alexis to come down from recovery. We have not been able to see her yet, because she had a crisis while she was in recovery and had to be taken back into surgery. Lorenzo and Stephen make certain that Alexis can share an ICU room with her father and that her pediatric team will be able to work from this special arrangement. Until they are able to move her into this room, I have been keeping my distance from Alex. I will not be with him in the room alone. After a few more hours, I have to admit that I am relieved he is ok. I never would want him to die. Not like this. He is giving me my space, and it helps that his family has not left his side. I pop in to check on him, but I mostly wait with my family in the private waiting room for news on Alexis. I begin to make my siblings go home to take care of their families. I promise to let them know something as soon as I know anything. I tell my parents and grandmother to go home too, but they refuse to leave my side. My father does, however, take Avery and Aren to the cafeteria for breakfast and to give them a change of scenery.

Hours later, I find myself hovering near the door to

Alex's room. I am floating in between my "normal self", the strong and fragile oxymoron, and now, my "new normal" self. The crying crazy-angry lady ready to tear someone's head off. The only thing that time has changed is my wanting Alex. I want his cool confidence and strong presence. I want him to comfort me. But I cannot bring myself to go into his room because I still do not trust myself. Alexis has been in recovery and has not been moved to the ICU room with her father. I am glad she was not there resting when he woke up screaming "Where is Alexis? Where is my daughter?" He had to be sedated before he reinjured himself. I was not there, but our boys were there and it really shook them. Lorenzo was there for them.

Now, I am peeking through the window in the door. Looking at Alex sleeping peacefully, I am now able to allow a little of his peace to seep into my pain scarred heart allowing a part of me to be repaired. Seeing my daughter well, that would really help this process. Instead, I have not heard anything about how she is. Stephen has been more than helpful, but I had to let him go home. He and Denere were here all night like my family, and they had to take care of their kids. I had to force them to go home. Denere promised they would return as soon as their evening nanny returned.

I am so grateful for all their support.

I was deep in a phone conference conversation with my sisters Maria and IsaMara, when I see a young man in a white lab coat being pointed in my direction by one of the nurses at the nurse's station. Is she pointing at me? I am still standing outside Alex's room. He is walking up to me. This tall and dark chocolate man-boy whose teeth were as white as a snow-capped mountain. Having made those observations, as if on cue, a slow sexy-ish smile creeps up on his face. He has the deepest dimples on each side, the smooth hollows are nature's eighth wonder of the world. Who is this man-boy? And why is he walking up to me? Do I know him? I expect him to keep walking past me, but he stops directly in front of me.

"Mrs. Sterling?"

"Yes?"

"I am Dr. Isaiah Osbourne."

That name sounds familiar. Where have I heard that name before? Hmmmm. This boy is someone's Dr.? Whose Dr is this dark chocolate-drop Doogie Howser? I am trying to think. I then notice I am smoothing down my hair as I think. What are you doing Mercey?

Who is checking for your wrecked ass, right now, anyways? He must see the confused look on my face because he decides to take me out of my confusion.

"I am Dr. Osbourne. I am the surgeon who operated on your daughter, Alexis."

My mouth falls open. Shouldn't I be asking him tons of questions? Nope. I am still standing there gaping like a foolish fish out of water, when he speaks again.

"Uh, yes. You probably want to know what is happening with Alexis?"

I begin to hear my sisters repeatedly trying to get my attention. "Mercey? Mercey? What is going on? Hello! Hello, Mercey? Who is that?" They are still on the phone. I mumble into the receiver. "Alexis' doctor just walked up. He is smiling so everything must good." I hang up the phone, surprising myself but I cannot take my eyes off this "doctor" standing in front of me.

"How old are you?" Yes, I asked him that. You have to understand that I have not been asleep except for those 2 or so hours of forced sedation and that was it for over 24 hrs.

He laughs, "Let's just say that I am old enough and

qualified enough to be here, and in my case, looks can be deceiving."

Yes, Very deceiving indeed. "I am sorry. I have been waiting so long to hear something about Alexis. What has been happening?" I cannot believe how tamed I sound. I really wanted to say, "Where the fuck have you been, you tall assed 12 yr old "doctor"? Why the hell have we not heard something about our child for nearly 16 hours?" But no, I just acted as if I was raised by my passive mama like I was, and yes, she raised me with some damn sense.

He gestures to the door to Alex's room; "Shall we step in here? This is your husband's room, isn't it?"

"Uh, he is my ex-husband, and yes." What? Yes, I did THAT, too. "I am not sure if he is awake since he had to be sedated earlier."

"Well, let us take a look then. I am sure he is anxious to hear about Alexis, as well."

What, is he handling me? Really? This is a trip! But what do I say, "Ok." Yeah, that is right! I say "Ok." Just like a good girl. Sheesh!

We walk into Alex's room, and he turns his head

towards me. He looks at me and he smiles. That $1 billion smile. He looks past me and sees Dr. Isaiah. He is still smiling but he looks confused, too. Good, it isn't just me. This dude looks too young, who is he fooling?

"Mr. and Ms. Sterling, I am Dr. Isaiah Osbourne, I apologize for the delay in meeting you. I stopped the nurses from relaying information, and I wanted to be the one to speak with you about Alexis' condition. I wanted to wait until she was stable to come down and answer any questions you both may have."

I am just staring at him. I cannot find the words to any of the questions I had only moments ago. I only shake my head.

He continues, "So has Stephen, Dr. Whitmore, answered all of your questions?"

"No, I am just..." I find my voice, but it sounds very raspy and raw. I close my mouth and I shake my head again.

"So how is she, Doc?" Alex asks.

"I would like to stress that she is in stable condition, and she has improved tremendously since she arrived.

As she sleeps her body is in recovery. To her credit, She is a little fighter."

"What exactly were her injuries? Stephen said that she had internal injuries." I am finally able to ask.

"That is correct. She did have internal bleeding in her stomach. Also, she has a broken clavicle, or collarbone, and her left wrist and right femur. Her left lung was punctured. There was also slight swelling on her brain. All in all, we expect her to fully recover. We were able to stop the bleeding and swelling, now we will watch for infection which is our greatest concern."

"Does she know that we are here? Is she in pain?"

"We have her heavily sedated, and she should not be feeling any pain. She is not conscious yet, but, as soon as she is ready to be moved, I understand that we will be moving her in here. You will most likely be the first people she will see when she comes to."

"Good." Alex mumbles. He then lets out a soft snore. I cannot believe he fell asleep. I want to thump him on his forehead.

Dr. Osbourne must have seen the annoyed look I was giving Alex and comes to his defense. "He has been sedated and is on a lot of pain medication as well. I am really surprised that he was awake for any of this conversation."

"You are probably right." He is staring at me. His eyes are penetrating, and they are beginning to make me feel uncomfortable.

"I am sorry, Ms. Sterling, but have we met before? I feel as if we have met somewhere before."

I clear my throat. "Eh-hmm. No, I do not think that we have." Because I would have definitely remembered such an encounter, but of course, fortunately, I kept that last comment to myself.

He smiles, as if he heard my thoughts, and says " I definitely remember seeing you before. I just cannot remember where. Where do you go to church?"

"I go to Hope Tabernacle UPC. Have you been there?" I reply.

"That must be it! I attend Bethesda Tabernacle UPC in South Tampa."

"Oh, Brother Hughes is your pastor?"

"Yes. I knew that I had seen you before. I would have

never forget such a sweet spirit."

"Hmmpfpfhhh. It wasn't such a "sweet" spirit a few hours ago. I am glad that you were the doctor here for my daughter, it comforts me to know that someone with like faith was with Alexis."

"That is how the Holy Spirit works. I was supposed to be off 2 hours before your daughter arrived, but I had to finish some chartwork before leaving. I just so happened to still be here. God is Good!"

"All the time!" I am smiling. I thank him again, I say goodbye. This is my first smile since this whole thing began.

I was so very relieved, I felt my face relax. I stopped grinding my teeth. My jaw loosened. My neck has relaxed. I continued to smile as I walked away from Dr. Isaiah. I just wonder why this had to happen to my family? I have a bad habit of questioning God's intentions when horrible things happen. This was bad. I know it could have been worse, but it wasn't. It was just what it was. I feel my frown returning and my jaw begins to tighten, as thoughts of Raemier creep back in.

Processing an injured Raemier took longer than

normal for the Tampa Police Department. They had to make sure she was able to be in lock up, and, that she did not need an extended stay in the hospital or the infirmary. She was hysterical at the beginning but had now become surprisingly quiet. Her breathing has become controlled and soft. She begins to whisper incoherently, and it sounds as if she is just babbling random words. She is whispering to no one. Tampa police chose to place her in a holding cell by herself with a posted guard checking on her every 20. The last thing the city needs is a dead inmate from negligence in their department. At the last check, Raemier was found in the corner of her cell curled up in the fetal position crying and pulling at her hair. The female guard checking on her tried futilely to get her to get up off the floor. In her report, she documents that Raemier was wanting to know the condition of the little girl inside the car.

Watching Alexis sleep so peacefully was too much for me. I keep checking her vitals on the monitors next to her bed. Perfect heart rhythm is still there. I am a raging storm. Everyone keeps telling me to pray. I just cannot do it. I have never felt so distant and far from God, than I do right now. I keep asking -- how could HE have let this happen to her? Why didn't

HE stop Raemier? Do I blame HIM or her? I know that these questions can be dangerous and can lead to walking a difficult path, but I still cannot help it. I have no one to confide these feelings to. My family would not understand. I would be under attack if my mother knew my faith is this low. Weak. Almost gone. It would return if only my baby would open her eyes and recognize me. If I were to know that she is 100% healed and back to normal, and not in any pain.

I walk back into Alexander and Alexis's hospital room from a walk/meditation I very much needed. I just had to get out of the room. I could not stand Alexander looking at me, waiting for me to speak to him. I do not want to say anything to him that I might regret. I do not know what to say and if I opened my mouth to say anything, everything wrong could come out. I just do not want to do or say anything to him. I come in with my head and eyes averted down and I see a pair of high heels standing next to Alexander's bed. I look up and I see a voluptuous, curvy female touching his shoulder gently and I throw my head back and gasp when I see it is Shenay. I have not seen her in years and now she is comforting a tearful Alexander, who straightens up immediately when he sees me standing there with my mouth wide open. I cannot process this.

I had no idea he was still in contact with her. She turns to face me and I immediately regret the grey Victoria's Secret tracksuit I put on this morning during my brief stop at home to shower and change.

"Mercey, how are you? I was so sorry to hear about Alexander's accident and then to find out about your daughter's status, I had to come see my old friends."

"Oh? How did you hear about this? I wasn't aware that you were still in touch with Alexander."

" I read Lorenzo's Facebook page, and I drove up from Ft. Lauderdale to see for myself how he is doing."

"Curious, Nay, why would you do that?"

"Despite how I was treated nearly 20 years ago by the both of you, I still think of you both fondly, and I would still consider both of you my friends."

"Funny, I would not think of us as friends, especially after not speaking to you for 17 years; nor to follow Lorenzo or any of us on Facebook; and certainly I would not have expected you to have driven 6 hours to see someone you have not spoken to in over 16 years."

"Hmmpfpfhhh, well, I have spoken to Alexander, I

speak with him every quarter, he manages my finances. I see Alexander is still doing his same old tricks, not exactly being transparent in his relationships is he? I guess I owe you congratulations, I see that you are engaged." She says as she nods her head at my hand and the obscene rock that is on it. I had forgotten that I put on my old engagement ring. "So, who is the lucky fellow?"

I look at Alexander he looks at me pleadingly, pleading for what? For me not to say it is his ring or for me to say that I still claim him? I begin to get angry again and he speaks for me.

"She wears my ring."

Shenay turns back to him quickly, I think she was in shock, she says, " You are going for a second try with Mercedes? I had no idea! Good for you two."

The words sound hollow and disingenuous. Now I am really angry, it appears that Shenay was hoping for another round with Alexander since his divorce. I never knew her to be crazy or delusional, so why on earth would she think that this was in the stars for her? I look at Alexander again. He takes his eyes off of me and he says, "Thank you Shenay, that she would even consider taking me back makes me the lucky one,."

"Oh, I imagine so." She says through what sounds like her clenched teeth. She turns on her heels and says " I guess I will leave you two to discuss, whatever."

She walks towards the door looks at me, from my head to my toes, again and shakes her head slightly.

"What is that supposed to mean?" I ask her as I look at Alexander.

"Hmmmpghff" she grunts and walks out the door.

I walk over to Alexander, who is not looking at me. I realize that I really do not care what he has to say and I turn back to go to my daughter's bedside.

"Mercedes."

I ignore him.

"Mercedes, please, it isn't what you are thinking." He says.

"I am not "thinking" anything. I just REALIZED that I do not care anymore."

"Don't say that."

"I have to say that, if it weren't for your inability to end things properly with girls/women in your life, we wouldn't even be here. Our daughter would not be seriously injured and in the hospital at the fucking age of 11! Alex, this baby has a fucking brain injury BECAUSE of YOU! This "we" is something I do not know nor understand what you expected from me. So did you string Shenay along, what, for just in case we do not make it? Are you so afraid of being alone that you keep cycling through the same women over and over for fucking decades!"

"That is not what I am doing. The only reason why she is a client of mine is when I first began my practice, I needed clients really bad, so I reached out to her and she accepted."

"You have been in contact with her for that long?"

"Yes."

"Why haven't you told me before now?"

"I knew that you would not approve."

"Damn right. The fact that there are things in your life you feel you must keep from me proves all of my suspicions. Bottom line, you aren't ready to give me the relationship I need and want."

There is only silence now, until.

"Mommy, please don't be mad at daddy."

I gasp, it was Alexis, and she is awake, I press the nurse's call button and I kiss my baby gently on her forehead. I couldn't ask for better timing than her opening her eyes at that very moment, it was exactly what we needed.

Two nurses rush into the room and Dr. Osborne was right behind them. He takes a pen flashlight and looks into her eyes. He smiles. I guess that is good news.

I feel Alex looking at us from his bed. I feel sorry for him, but I quickly go back to being indifferent. He can stay on his side of the room and think about what he has done. I will not let him off the hook for Shenay. Not now, he has it too easy. He can sweat it out, that is, if he even cares. I do not care about what he is thinking nor feeling. My daughter has returned to me, she is alert and is talking like normal. Her brothers made it back in time to keep her busy. Life is almost good, again.

"Daddy, when can we all go home?" She asks

Alexander.

Aren, Avery, and Alexis all look over to Alexander's side of the room, where he looks back over at them, he smiles slightly and sighs, "that is up to our team of doctors and how well we heal." As soon as he says that the physical therapist walks into the room to begin his therapy. He closes his partition off on his side of the room with the curtain, and we soon hear Alex groaning in pain as he stretches his limbs and muscles. I hope that it hurts a little more than I should hope for.

I turn my attention back to my babies and smile. As I look at each one, I feel so blessed. I finally offer up a soft "Thank you, Jesus!"

"You aren't what I expected, you aren't who I thought you were." I say to Alex finally. I decided to take advantage of the time we have while Alexis is out of the room getting more scans.

"I do not know what you mean, Mercey."

"I thought you had matured and were ready for a real relationship with me. I had no idea that you were stringing along Shenay, in the background for some 15 plus years! I cannot believe I fell for you again! I would never have accepted your proposal. Not now, not ever we are over!"

"Wait! Do not be too rash. I admit that I was less than open and honest to Shenay, but I have never lied to either of you!"

"Lies by omission is still a lie."

"You never asked. I never thought to bring it up. I didn't think you'd care. It has only been business with her."

"Business? She says that you were her friend. The hurt on her face when you told her that we were back together said something very different to me. At the risk of sounding juvenile, I must say that I am well over you and your lying ass."

"Don't say that it is over, Mercey. I love you. It is only you whom I want."

"Just shut up. Shut your fucking mouth!"

"Mercey. Mercey don't!"

My heart cannot handle the disappointment. My heart is closing him off. I am on full alert, numbing, and in protection mode. All I want to do is run, flee from

Alexander Sterling.

Loving Alexander is to love pain and chaos.

Loving Alexander brings confusion.

He is a double-minded, selfish bitch-boy, who does not know what love is.

Shenay walks back into my life, and I realize there was no closure. Not for her, for me, for him. You would have thought that with all the time that has passed, we would have been mature enough to have reached closure. I certainly should have made sure of it. I will make sure it happens this time; but, not necessarily for this "relationship" because this relationship is now dead.

Who can believe that it was only 72 hours ago that I was falling back in love with my ex-husband, and we were happy, very happy. Now, we are taking up residence in the hospital with my daughter and the same ex having nearly lost their lives in a senseless violent act of a jealousy by a jilted lover. I cannot shake the feeling that if Alexander were completely healthy, we would have reconciled and my current feelings would have been long gone. We would have fucked our way back to happiness, and all would be well. We have now been unified in our fight against Raemier. This saddens me more. This cheapens what I thought we had. No, what I had wished, we had. I wanted us to have been more than just awesome magical sex.

Raemier has a visitor, and a very angry one at that - Raemier's mother, Mama Patti or Dr. Patrice Williamson, MD (psychiatrist). Mama Patti received a phone call from Mrs. Janeese Sterling-Roth, informing her of what had happened to Alexander and Alexis, not to mention to her grandsons Adrian and Andre. Patti is furious to have heard all of this from Janeese. Firstly, because her daughter chose not to come to her in her time of need; and secondly, Raemier's involvement with Alexander which in her opinion, has ruined her daughter's life once again. Not that Raemier is completely blameless in all of this, which is what has her the most furious. Raemier, actually attempted to kill Alexander and his daughter! What on earth was going through her mind? The answer to that question is exactly what she is here to find out now. Is her daughter well? A shackled Raemier is brought into the small room and is sat down in front of her mother. Patti is aware of how gingerly her daughter is being handled by the guards. Patti notices the neck brace and sling on her daughter's left arm. The extent of her injuries is unknown to Patti, but, she tries to focus on Raemier's eyes and not the superficial scratches, cuts, and bruises on her face. Raemier sits down carefully and keeps her eyes from meeting her mother's stern gaze. Raemier feels like a kid in the principal's office. Raemier speaks first, in a barely audible whisper, "How is Alexis? Is she ok?"

Patti clears her throat, "She will live, no thanks to you."

"Mother, I did not know that was her. She looked so grown up. Her hair was straightened. It is never straightened..."

"Be quiet, child." Patti spits at her daughter. Painfully aware that their conversation may be recorded, she attempts to keep Raemier from further incriminating herself.

Raemier jumps when she hears the anger in her mother's voice. "Mother, I...."

"Not another word, Rae. You listen to me. Why didn't you call or come see me when the boys were arrested? And when you were feeling so out of control? Why did I have to hear about your divorce and everything else from Janeese Sterling?"

"What Mom? Is that why you are so angry at me?! Because you found out from Janeese? Or, is it because I have embarrassed you once again? None of this has to do with you."

"You are my adult child and of course I am concerned about what happens to you."

"Since when, do you care?"

"Rae! Where is this coming from?"

"I tried to call you when I left Alex. You did not return my call."

Patti tried to think of when Raemier may have called her recently. She could not recall any phone calls missed from her daughter. She does remember talking to Lucinda, her other daughter, and mentioning that Raemier and the twins were staying with her temporarily. Patti admits to herself, she did not inquire why the boys were with Lucinda, but she is sure that Lucy did not say that Rae had left Alex indefinitely. Patti reasons that it is difficult to keep up with comings and goings in her seven children's lives. It does not help that they are connected to their father's three other children, as if seven children weren't enough. He needed ten children like he needed a hole in his head. Patti, you are displacing and digressing from the issues at hand. Rae. Stay focused on Rae. She thinks she embarrasses you. How can you get through to her? My standing in the psychiatric community is of no consequence when it comes to my children. So, now to the task at hand, determining if Raemier is competent.

Time is passing by so slowly at the hospital. The days run into each other. Waiting for all clear to go home. Watching Alex and Alexis go for different therapies and tests is causing me to feel selfish. I just want to go home and sleep in my own bed, bathe in my own tub or shower. The staff here at the hospital has been very accommodating and helpful trying to keep me and my sons, who are not patients, comfortable as we stay with our loved ones in residence. I had two fruit baskets delivered to the nurse's station as a thank you gift for them. I think I need to set up a lunch for them before we leave. I have a cousin who has a catering business, I think I will set that up while I am waiting. While I am thinking of arranging the lunch, I pick up my phone and shoot my cousin, Rod, a text, there it's done. The lunch will come in at 2 p.m. today. Alex is brought back into the room and as he is wheeled past me, he reaches for my hand, I recoil and move quickly away from him. It was awkward because the nurse that was there saw the exchange and quickly looked away. I am embarrassed for both of us.

"I am sorry.", I say.

"It's ok. You aren't ready."

"I was apologizing to the nurse."

"We have to talk about this soon."

I look at the nurse, he wheels Alexander to his bed and helps him into it, and quickly leaves the room. Now we are alone, Alexis will be out of the room for at least another hour.

"We embarrassed him."

"Yes."

"Ok. What do you want to say?" I ask.

"We have to get back on track.".

"We have too much in the way, I do not know if we can."

"We can get rid of the garbage. We have to."

"It isn't that simple. We have real issues, not so easily

cast off."

"Raemier will pay for this."

"Will she? It sounds as if she is working on an incompetent angle. Even Stephen said, "she wasn't 'there' when he saw her in the car.""

"Well, that is his opinion and it will not stop us from seeking the maximum. She must pay for nearly killing my child."

"Ok. And what about Shenay?"

"What about her? I don't want that girl."

"She didn't see it that way."

"I do not care about what she saw. It isn't like that."

"I care. You owe her closure and the bluntness of how it really is. How you really feel. No secrets."

"When I do that, where does that leave us?"

"There is no 'us', anymore."

"How can I fix that? What can I do?"

"Nothing. I do not trust you. You have not changed. In my eyes, you are the same selfish boy you have always been. I cannot trust my heart with you."

"Mercey. I will never hurt you again. I love you. I want you."

"Damn right, you won't hurt me again. You will not have the opportunity again because I will not let you."

Alexander begins shaking his head. He sighs deeply twice and then he looks at me again. Tears are in his eyes.

I find myself just looking at him. I feel nothing. Not sympathy, empathy, nor sadness. I feel numb. That isn't good either, I know. I look away. Then I turn to leave the room. Since my daughter isn't here, there is nothing here for me. I decide to leave Alex alone with reality.

Forget Alexander's reality. I am dealing with my own reality. I am hurting and I want to retreat into my room and never come out. I am saddened by the loss of Alexander. I need and want his love. Why am I punishing myself by ending things with him? This must be how drug addicts or smokers feel when they quit "cold turkey". Is it even more sad that I just compared our relationship to drugs? Sad. Just Sad. I need to pray. I find my way back home to my room, my sanctuary. I hear a small knock on my door and as I turn to open it I see my Avery. In my need to shut myself in, I did not know that anyone was home. I did not bother to check.

"Hi mom, how are daddy and Alexis?"

"Hi baby! They are fine. I just needed to come home and relax a little."

"Aren and I are going to head out to the school for gym time. Do you need us to get you anything, while we are out?"

"Awww aren't you sweet? Yes, you can bring me home some gelato, coffee flavored. Here, take my bank card."

"Ok. We will stop at Fresh Market on our way home. Should we get anything for dinner?"

"Oh yes. Get some steaks for me to put on the grill and fresh Asparagus, onions, and bell peppers. Can you remember all that?"

"Yeah Ma. I got it!"

"Ok. Well, let me know when you are headed home so that I can start the grill."

"I will. Mom? Are you ok?"

"Yes babe, I am. Why do you ask?"

"Well, Aren and I just got off the phone with dad and he is very upset. He says that you two have broken up."

One, two punches to my gut!

"Uh, yes, I have ended things with your father, again."

Avery looks disappointed. I hate that my son is saddened by the fact that his father and I are no longer together.

"So, how does that make you feel?" I ask my son.

"Well, I was upset when he told us. Why did you end things this time?"

"I ended things because I do not trust your father to be selfless enough. I ended things because I do not feel it is safe for me to invest more of my life with him. He has not matured enough to be good for my needs." I tried to make it simple for my son to understand.

"But, is that really true, mom? He has changed. You were happy with him this time. I saw you smiling every day. It was real again."

"He was keeping secrets from me. It was shady."

"Ok. Well, I hope you are ok. So, are you… Ok?"

"What? You were about to say something else."

"It's nothing. I gotta go, Aren is waiting for me."

I grab my son and hug him tightly. I have a lump in my throat the size of a mountain. I hold my tears back, I am about to be alone soon, I can let them flow freely after my sons leave.

"Be careful out there." I croak to Avery.

"You be careful here."

"I am about to get into the tub and do a little pampering."

I rub his head and send him on his way.

"Do you remember the PIN for the bank card?"

"Yes, Mom, I got it!"

I watch Avery walk down the hallway to the landing above the stairs. His head is being held low. I made him sad. He will soon be ok, though.

I turn around and closed the door behind me. I go

into my ensuite and start the water in my tub. I light candles and get bath salts to add to the water. I add oil and parfum the fragrances begin to fill the entire room. It is heavenly to my senses. Bright floral notes wrap around me as I test the water's heat. It is perfect. I turned on the tub's heater to maintain the temperature in case I fall asleep. I attach my bath air pillow, for prime relaxation. As I wait for the tub to fill up, I begin to think. Should I forgive Alex? Should I be more patient with him? Cut him some slack? No, if I do not stand up for myself, who will? Alex is wrong hiding his continued communication with Shenay all these years. I thought she was gone from his life, and but a distant memory. I have had no fear of her, I just know that closure is needed for her to get him out of her system. In order for her to regain her life, she needs a clean break, or closure will never come. It is especially true if she has been waiting for Alexander to resume a relationship with her which is so sad to me.

Finally, I can give my body the release it needs, I climb into the tub and let the water envelope me hugging my shoulders and encircling my neck and I settle in for a good soak. I let the dam burst and I cry. Tears pour from my eyes and I do not know how to end the flow. I cry for my daughter and for my future. I cry to let go of Alexander. I cry for the love I do not have to take us to the next level. I cry for the "I told you so's" my mom can now say. I cry because I am alone and I was ok with being alone until he woke up my feelings again. I do not want it. I want to be in the relationship I thought we had. As long as the façade was strong, the fiction was fine. Why did he have to put two flaws in it, those two bitches -- Shenay and Raemier. I submerge my head in the hot water. I reemerge and take in a long deep, cool breath and I begin to feel better. The phone begins to ring. I am not interested in getting out of my watery haven. I reason that it could be the hospital calling me about Alexis. I stand up and grab my robe and step out of the tub. Fortunately, there is a phone on the wall in my ensuite. I answer it just in time.

"Hello?"

"Hey." It is his voice and it makes my stomach fall. Why is he calling me?

"What is wrong? Is Alexis ok?"

"Nothing is wrong. Yes, she is fine. She is sleeping."

"Ok, good. What do you want?"

"Why are you so hostile? I did not call to start or continue conflict, before 'this' happened we were in a great place, I cannot let it end like this."

"Yes, but 'this' did happen."

"It wasn't my fault."

"You're right, you weren't driving the car, but your messiness fueled the fever behind it."

"My messiness?"

"Yes."

"Wow, how can we move past this?"

"I, 'we' cannot. I do not have enough love in me to wait for you to mature enough emotionally to be what I need, and you still do not know what I need in a man to be that for me 100%, and I do not have the energy to teach you."

"You do not love me enough?"

"Sadly, no. Look, Alex, I was in the tub, I want to return to it."

"Oh, ok. I will let you go. I was calling you to let you know that I am going home today."

"Already?"

"Yes. I am having the boys pick me up and take me home."

"Did they know already? They went to the gym, then the store."

"Yes, I called them first."

"Oh. Well alright. Tell Alexis I will be back at the hospital tonight and I will spend the night with her."

"I talked to Dr. Osbourne about getting her home soon with her own medical crew and he said that could be done. We would have to bring her home with medical transport, basically an ambulance for her safety and care. To administer her oxygen and watch the lung."

"Wow how much will that cost us?"

"It will be a small fortune, what our insurance doesn't cover, I have it covered. I explained to them that since I will no longer be in the hospital, I do not feel comfortable leaving my young daughter there all alone. It is something that is covered by our plan, and we must have it for our daughter."

"Will this 'around the clock care' include a doctor

along with the nurses? I have the space here to accommodate the extra people."

"They shouldn't need to stay there, but the spare room can be their break room. Dr. Osbourne said she could perhaps be home by Monday. In two days. I wanted to let you know the good news. Now get back to your bath, I will see you in a few."

"Wait, what?"

He hung up the phone. I am left standing there holding the phone talking to a deadline. What did he mean, that he'll "see me in a few"??

I do not care. I get back to my tub and I test the water. It is tepid, even with the heater on, I release the valve to let some water out, and then I turn on the hot water to replace the water that was lost. I make a mental note to have the heater checked out. I test the water and it is perfect again. I get back into the water. I start thinking about what I will need to do to get the spare bedroom next to Alexis's room ready for the medical team. I will need a second bed just in case they would like to lie down, along with a coffee brewer, a juice and water stocked fridge. I will need to call my internet provider to have the signal/speed boosted for the extra equipment that will be used for her care. I will also need to find out how long Alexis will need the in-home care to determine how long my home will be home base for this team. I really do not care, as long as she is home and safe, that is what I need for my peace of mind. Alex knew that, and he made it happen.

I must have dozed off because I was awakened by someone scrubbing my shoulders. I open my eyes and it is Alex with his one arm in a sling and the other holding my bathing poof smiling at me. I look up at him trying to cover myself with …., what? Nothing! All the bubbles are gone, and why am I trying to cover myself for modesty? He has literally seen it all millions of time. I am trying to process why Alex is in my bathroom? Shouldn't he be home recuperating? I finally determine I can find my voice and I ask. "Why are you here?" I stop his hand from rubbing my back, and I begin to stand. He stops me.

"I told you I would see you soon. Let me wash your back."

"No."

"Why not?"

"I do not want this. This time, I cannot be persuaded."

I begin to cry. This has me so miserable. I really want to fall into his arms and have him hold me. I know that I cannot trust him. I just bury my face into my hands, and I cry. My cry becomes a sob and now I cannot stop.

"Mercey, why are you doing this to us? We were doing so well."

I stifle a sob and say. "We were doing well, until your shit nearly killed Alexis and you. And, then, I find that you and Shenay are still seeing each other."

"Wait. Shenay and I aren't seeing each other like that."

"I know that you think that, but she obviously had another take on your relationship. I have to be with someone I can trust, who can protect me, and not be the cause of what is hurting me."

"I can be that."

I shake my head, "Sadly, you cannot. You never have been that for me. If you'd ended things with Raemier properly, she would not be trying to get revenge on you. If you had ended things with Shenay properly, she would not be wasting her time on trying to get you back. You just do not handle your shit well. You are ... I have no more time for your shitty life. You have wasted enough of my life, and I need and want more than just your golden tongue and deceptive platinum dick. I want better."

"So, it's like that, huh?"

"Yes."

"I love you; I will always love you. There is no mess there."

"I love you, too."

"Then, let's work together, make this right for both of us."

"You need to worry about your twins and our children, and you have to heal, so your hands are full."

"Yeah, Heal."

I look at him and I see this is hurting him deeper than I expected. I open my mouth to speak, he begins first.

"I never would have thought Raemier would react this way. Clearly, she must have had a breakdown of some sort since she left me. I am not making excuses for her, but she can't be right in the head. Stephen told me, he spoke with Raemier and he thinks she thought I had another female in the car. She was very upset after finding out that it was Lexi. I do not know."

"That is what I am talking about. You do not give anyone enough time to have complete closure when things are ended. You can't just hop into the next relationship, and this is why I have to put the brakes on this whole situation."

"I understand what you are saying. I just do not want to end what we have started again. I will give you and me the time we need."

"We can be friends."

"Can we? Really be friends, knowing that we could be so much more?"

"You need to be alone and function that way."

"Yep. Ok get out of this tub because you are making it hard for me to just be your friend."

I look at him and I blush, remembering that I have been sitting in my tub this whole time.

"Ok. Hand me my robe and that towel." I point to the wall where they are hanging. He walks to them, and I stand up and step out of the tub. He turns around and he looks at me, standing there, I think I started something. I just shrug as I reach for the towel. I cover myself and begin drying off. Poor Alexander, he looks as if all of the air has left the building. Perhaps, this will give him something to work for. I take my robe from him as well and I put it on. It is a short, silk robe and I walk quickly into my closet and shut the door behind me so that I can get dressed. I work fast, because if I know Alex (and I do know Alex), he will come through that door in 5-4-3-2-1 or maybe, in 1-2. The door opens and he walks in. I guess he isn't as fast as I thought. I smile to myself.

"I will be right out." I say to him. "Let me get dressed."

"That is why I am in here; I am trying to stop you. I can't get your image out of my mind. I want you so bad, Mercey!"

"Do me a favor and sit your lusty, crippled behind down somewhere!" I laugh at the wounded look he is giving me. I continue getting dressed. I slip a long maxi dress over my head and let my robe fall to the floor. He steps closer and tries to stop the cascade of fabric from covering me, and he reaches forward too fast wincing in pain. He is doing too much. I attempt to steady him, and I wasn't quite prepared to receive his full weight and we both fall to the floor. We both laugh.

"Yeah, well, it was a thought." He says.

"I shouldn't have teased you."

"Were you teasing me? I thought that was a full-on invitation."

"No Alex, I meant what I said about stopping this."

He sits himself up using his good arm, and winces in pain.

"Come on." I stand up. "Let's get out of here." I offer him a hand, helping him to his feet. I keep my arm around his waist, and we leave my ensuite and we enter my bedroom. I help him sit in a wingback chair. And go back to my closet and get a pair of panties to put on. I come back into the room and find him lying in my bed. He looks winded.

"When was the last time you took a pain pill?"

"It was a while ago."

"Do you have any with you?"

"Yes, in my pocket."

"Well, you should take one, now."

I leave my room and head downstairs to get him a bottle of water. On my way back upstairs, I see Avery and Aren outside on the lanai trying to start the grill. I step outside to show them how.

"Hey, ma" Aren says

"Having trouble?"

"Yeah, I forgot how to work this thing."

"Did you turn on the gas?"

"Ahh that's it!"

I turn the knob and I take the lighter from his hand as I start the fire.

"We will cook the steaks and get dinner ready. You and dad can take it easy."

"Uh-huh." I look at him and Avery, I see what they are trying to do. They are trying to ambush my breakup with their father.

Avery says, "Mom, can dad and the twins stay here while he finishes recovering? Since he doesn't have anyone at his house to help him out."

I do not answer but I notice their pleading eyes, I just turn away from my sons and sigh. I roll my eyes at them and take the water upstairs to Alex.

How can I? I do not want to say no, but he is deliberately trying to ignore my wishes for a break. He is a master manipulator.

When I reach my room, I see that he has fallen asleep. I wake him gently and hand him his water. I open the medicine bottle next to him and read how many pills he should take. I hand him one capsule according to what the label says. He takes the pill and drinks all of the water.

"The boys want to know if I'd let you and the twins stay here while you're recuperating, was that your idea?"

I look at him side-eyed and watch for his reaction.

"I wouldn't mind that at all. I mentioned it to them in the car. They were concerned about me living alone and having no one there to help me."

"Listen, you aren't exactly an invalid!"

"No, but I need help getting dressed and eating. Will you help undress and feed me, Mercey?"

I sigh, "You should have done the asking instead of having our sons doing your dirty work. If this was your plan from the beginning, you could have asked me when we were on the phone."

"And not have the chance to sweeten the offer?"

"Sweeten it, how?"

"Well, I tried to."

"Hmpfff. Whatever you say. Dammit Alex you are trying to manipulate me, and I won't stand for it!"

"Wait, wait, wait, Mercey. That is not what I am trying to do. I am just having a little fun with you!"

"Fun for you, at my expense!"

"No, stop, you are taking this all the wrong way."

"So what? I am supposed to play your nurse, be at your beck and call 24/7? Forgive me that does not sound like fun to me! Especially with Alexis coming home with a medical team staying here. I have to have Yarra come and clean this house somehow before Monday!"

"Come here, and sit down, please. I am not trying to make your life difficult. It was just an idea. You can say no. It won't be a big deal, if you do. I will be ok."

"Do you think I have a problem telling you no?"

"No, I definitely do not think so."

I shake my head and sigh. "You can stay."

"Really? You are ok with my staying?"

"Look, don't start asking those kinds of questions. You may cause me to change my mind. I said yes, so just leave it alone."

"Alright, cool."

"Yeah, cool."

Just then, there is a knock at my bedroom door. I opened it, it was Aren.

"Hey, mom. The food is ready."

"Ok. We will be right down. Help your father downstairs, he just took a pain medication. I cannot have our new houseguest falling down the stairs."

Aren smiles at the news. We both help Alex out of my tall bed. He was trying to sit up. I put my hand under his good arm and helped him lift himself off the bed. Aren is helping him with his legs. Alexander appears to be steady, and I let Aren finish helping his father. I go ahead of them, down the stairs because I want to make sure there is a complete meal. I let two teenagers make dinner, after all. I see Avery spooning mashed potatoes onto plates next to grilled asparagus, corn, and the steaks. I take four glasses out of the cabinet and begin to pour sweet tea for everyone. I begin to think about Alexis and how happy we all will all be when she gets home on Monday. I wonder if she will need a special diet prepared, and right before I set into full on "worry wart" mode, I hear Avery say.

"The steaks came out more medium, than medium-rare, but, I did ok for my first time, sorry"

"That is ok. I appreciate your efforts. You gave me a break taking care of dinner for all of us." I say.

"Mom, the elevator is sweet!" Aren is saying as he walks into the kitchen supporting his father.

"Oh yeah? I forgot that we had that, we never use it. Good thing, it still works." Avery replies.

"That is great. I was wondering how we were going to get Alexis upstairs." I say.

"You forgot there was an elevator? You all have been living in this house for more than 12 years, I do not even live here anymore, and I knew there was an elevator. I used it to get upstairs in the first place. There was no way I could have used the stairs, in my condition!" Alexander says.

"You also worked with the design team when we constructed this house. I was pregnant with Aren then. Baby brain is my excuse." I say.

"You know that you can also set Lexi and team up in the 2 bedrooms downstairs? That would be better if they have to bring large equipment in." Alexander asks.

"Yeah, but I thought that Lexi would want to be in her own room. I guess we will find out which would be better when someone calls me to set everything up." I replied.

Aren and Avery both say, "We should eat."

Aren continues, "Before the food gets too cold."

"Yeah." Avery adds.

"It looks delicious, Avery." Alexander says.

"Thanks, but both of us did it." Avery states.

"You both make a great team. Always remember that. We are always better together." Alexander says to them, while staring at me.

Taking a sip of iced tea, I raise my eyebrows at Alexander and say, "Stop it."

"What? I am talking to the boys; I want them to remember to stay close." Alexander says sheepishly.

"Yeah, right, you say it to them as you stare at me." I roll my eyes at him. "Whatever Alex."

"Mooooom… please." Aren says.

"What?" I ask.

"Let's just enjoy the dinner. Avery almost lost his eyebrows preparing for us." Aren teases, he begins cutting Alex's steak for him.

"I did not!" Avery exclaims.

I get busy preparing for Alexis' arrival. I call my HVAC company to have the air purifier serviced, all ducts cleaned, and filters changed.

It has been a week since Alexis arrived home. The house is abuzz with activity from her medical team milling about, Alexander working in my home office holding meetings, sharing my bedroom (I will tell you about that later) and the boys doing their usual. After Alexander got Adrian and Andre out of detention three weeks ago, they spent some time with Lorenzo then, Alexander brought them here. The house is full and there is a lot to get use to. The twins are the sweetest I have ever seen them, and since their mother is locked up, they are happy to be here with their siblings and father. Andre even said that he wants nothing to do with his mother, since she tried to kill his sister and father. It is unforgivable to him. Adrian hasn't said much about the incident. As long as they remain respectful in my house, I am ok with the current arrangement.

Speaking of the twins, there were no charges brought against them, because they were not Mirandized. They are minors and they were interrogated without their parents or their counsel. Lorenzo made sure it was all thrown out. Alexander is taking them for therapy to Ms. Patti, their grandmother, to make sure they are handling the changes that are taking place in their young lives which may be affecting their mental health.

Alexis has been "altered" from the whole experience. She'd been having frequent nightmares and has to wear soft restraints to keep from removing her IV, drain tubing, and catheter. She had removed them twice in her sleep so the medical staff recommended she be restrained. Through it all, she is still my sweet little girl, in spite of all the trauma. She still cannot reconcile how or why Raemier did this to her. None of us, may also never understand either. Raemier still insists she did not realize that it was Lexi in the car. Lexi's swelling has decreased tremendously, and we are now able to see our little girl's features returning to normal. She has also begun smiling again.

When she returned home her nurse handed me a small baggie and inside of it were Alexis' diamond jewelry which was removed when she was rushed into surgery. We had all forgotten all about them. Thankfully, the hospital staff were honest and made sure that it was all returned. Unfortunately, her favorite headband/tiara was destroyed in the collision.

Now back to Alex sharing my bed. I only have 7 bedrooms and with the additional bodies in residence my huge home is at capacity. It has been awkward and frustrating having to be his nurse and having to fight off his evening advances and it's getting exhausting. If his arm wasn't in a sling, I would be in trouble! He's like an octopus with his one good arm. He insists on sleeping in the nude; and, he always ends up on my side of the bed with Alejandro pressed against my back. If his body wasn't broken already, I would have pushed him out of my bed. He has 4 broken ribs and even that is not stopping him from trying to 'get some puma'. To use the word Insatiable would be an understatement. However, I will not lie, he may be weakening my resolve. The problem is, how long will I be able to just give him just pussy without the entanglement of giving him my heart? I decided that I will test it tonight. I crave closeness and limited intimacy. I know, no self-control. Who fucking cares? I will be selfish this time. This sex is about my needs.

Later that evening, after taking care of Alexis and after dinner with the boys, I brought Alex upstairs to get him ready and undressed him for bed. I helped him into bed.

"Lay on your back" I instructed him.

He looked at me inquisitively, I climbed in the bed next to him. I lifted my dress and straddled his hips. I put Alejandro inside Mercia, and I slowly began to ride Alexander.

He just closes his eyes and moans. "Oh my god."

"Shhh." I just want his organ, if he remains silent, I can give myself to just the act, detached from him. Yes, this is where I am. Cold. Numb. Detached. Powerful. As I ride Alex, silently, I feel him trying to pump underneath me. I open my eyes and look at him and shake my head. I am in control of this situation and he is just the tool for my pleasure. He looks hurt, as he begins to understand.

My inner muscles begin to flutter then begins the clapping of ecstasy. I breathe deeply and continue the climb. I am chasing the exhausted feeling of complete satisfaction. I peek to see if I am hurting him physically, but nope, he's still there, looking at me. With his dumb face. In the second climax he finally speaks.

"May I cum?" He asks.

Crash. Boom. Ruined my mood. I look at him again.

Sigh heavily. "Sure, go ahead." I begin to remove myself from him.

He gasps. "Wait. No. Let me."

"What? You thought that this was for you?" I ask.

"No, I get it. This was for you. I just - we have never done this before."

"You're right. I loved you before. Now this is what it is. I thought that you should know what you are asking for when you solicit sex from me. I figured that I could show you better than I could tell you. You wouldn't get it otherwise."

I begin riding him again and quicken my pace and I climax again. Power going to my head I say "Cum."

He does. I climb off of him and I walk to my ensuite and turn on the shower. I return to the bedroom with a wet towel, and I toss it on his chest.

"Clean yourself off."

I return to the shower and get in. As I wash myself, I begin to lament my actions. I forgot the condom. Oh well, our chemicals are mingled in my reservoir, I will be absorbing him. Intimacy was happening anyway.

Mental note, pick up condoms for next time.

He was still awake when I returned to the bedroom. I can see that he wants to talk. I sigh, climb on my side, and I face him. "What?"

"I have never in my life been fucked before. Not even when you were angry with me." He says. "I did not like it."

"What do you expect from me? I have told you that you will not have my heart again. But here you are in my bed naked, night after night begging me for some ass. Nightly penis pressing on my back, I am a woman with needs, too."

"Not like this."

"So, what, you don't want me to do this again?"

"Not like that." He stares at me. "I need your touches, kisses, and eyes, you won't even look at me. I need us to connect."

"Sorry. No." I turn over, my back to him. I stare at the wall. I hear him huff and he remains silent. I resolved to get myself a non-verbal sex toy. After the multiple orgasms, sleep was illusive. Why was I feeling guilty? I turn back to face Alexander, and he is still facing me with open eyes. It startles me.

"Can't sleep either?" He asks.

"No, you want some more pussy?"

"Seriously, Really?"

"Yes."

"You seriously did not listen to me before?"

"That is what you do to me all of the time." I look under the sheets and see the state of Alejandro. "I see it's a 'yes' get on your back. Do you have condoms?"

"No and no. I'm straight on detached sex."

I get on my knees and begin to make my way to his side, pulling my night shirt off. "Look, I will be naked too. Do you need me to put on some music? Are you serious about not having any condoms? As much as you have been trying me for sex, without having any condoms?" Rolling him on his back, gently.

He sucks his teeth in defiance, "There are some in my bag."

"Mmhmm, well we will use them next time." I climb on his hips, placing my hands behind me on his thighs.

I raise my hips and allow him to position himself. I slide down, he shifts and begins to pump with my rocking. He stares at me, I avert my eyes to his chest watching his rhythmic breathing. I match his breath's intake (Yes, I still want to connect in some way, I'll give him that.) I smile at my silly thoughts. That must have been a bone thrown at his fragile ego.

"You're smiling."

"Yeah."

"Are you enjoying this?"

"Very much, I enjoy the sex." I lean forward and cover his eyes and mouth with both hands. He shakes his head.

"Hey! You said that you wanted me to touch you."

"You know what I meant."

"I am trying not to hurt you. You have broken ribs. We aren't even supposed to be doing any of this."

"Let me worry about my pain. The only thing that is hurting me is the fact that you are using me as a piece of meat." Ego is hurt. Got it.

I place my hands on either side of his torso and lay

gently on his chest. Skin to skin. "How is that?"

"Better." I feel him wrap his good arm around my back grabbing my ass. He does a sharp intake and grunts in pain. I sit up quickly.

"No, come back. The reach was too ambitious for my ribs, it shifted them. Come back, please."

I rock my hips and return to our skin-to-skin position. I feel his heart beating rapidly. I begin to sweat. I whisper, "This is good?" It is both a question and a statement.

"Very. No matter how this is right now, I will take it. There will never be a time where I will turn you down. In any capacity. I do love you, Mercedes. It can only explain how we are drawn to each other."

"It's just lust."

"Nah. Queen, This. (Pump) Is. (pump, pump) Us. (pump, pump, pump)"

"My point is proven."

"Look at me."

"Nah, king ding dong."

After the magic. Sleep is waiting for its turn to claim me. I wake to a knock on the bedroom door.

"Who?" Alex asks.

"It's Avery. May we go to the gym?"

"Who is 'we'?" Alex asks.

"Aren, Adrian, Andre, and myself?"

"Uh, Avery, come in." I say. My oldest son walks into the room slowly. I begin, "I do not know about taking the twins anywhere without an adult present."

"But mom, they aren't in jail anymore. It isn't fair for them to be cooped up like this."

"Excuse me, son, they are grounded. Their punishment is that they go nowhere without an adult." Alex says. "After your mother said no, since when do you have anything else to say? Keep it up, you can join them in their punishment."

"No sir, I'm Sorry mommy, sorry daddy."

Boy, did I miss having Alexander co-parenting at home. "Uh huh. If it is so important, why don't you all go play on the basketball court in the back yard or even use the home gym to work out?"

"Yes, you all do that instead." Alex agrees. "None of you need to go out anywhere."

"Yes, ma'am, yes sir. Am I on restriction? I wanted to take Brianna to the movies tonight."

I look at Alex, he shakes his head. "No, just watch yourself. Next time you feelin' froggy and decide to leap remember, you have more to lose than they do. Fight your own battles and better decide what hills are worth dying on. Andre and Adrian are paying consequences for their actions. It makes me proud that you are willing to step up for your brothers, but never to me or your mom. We will always do what is best for each of you. Just because they weren't charged for what they did, does not mean that they escaped judgment. I am their judge and I decide when they are out of trouble. When they are indeed free."

"Yes sir." Avery hangs his head and turns to leave. "So, ya'll just gonna be naked in bed all day?"

I gasp, Alex guffaws and throws his pillow at the boy. Hitting him, softly, in the back of his head.

"Get your ass out of here!" He laughs.

"Avery!" I exclaim.

He giggles and closes the door behind him. I look at Alex and he is still laughing, holding his sides, and wincing slightly. I roll over to get out of bed.

"Where are you going?" Alex asks.

"I am going to shower, fix our breakfast, and check on Lexi. You need to eat with your meds."

"Don't be gone too long. Let Lexi know that I will be in this afternoon and continue reading to her. We are reading "Harry Potter and The Half Blood Prince". I really like the story. Who knew? I haven't read to the kid since she was much younger and I lived here. I miss it, I missed all of it."

"Yeah." I continue to the ensuite, turn on the shower and step in. I turn on the rain head above and stand in the center letting the water cascade over me, saturating my chaotic head. Willing myself not to cry. I lose because, my tears fall, mixing with the shower water. I remain silent so that I can have this private moment.

After breakfast, I go to Lexi's room. Lexi is awake when I enter. The hospital bed sits in the middle of her lounge/sitting area. She is having her vitals checked by a nurse. Her little brown eyes light up when she sees me.

"Mommy! I am so happy to see you. You look so pretty and relaxed." She says.

"I do? Well, it has to be because my baby girl is doing better and is home with her whole family. That can only be the reason," I say as I look at the nurse. The nurse nods her head after checking Lexi's blood pressure and temperature. She goes to the terminal and looks at the monitors behind the bed.

"Mrs. Sterling, Alexis' respiratory therapist will be in for therapy in about a half hour. Dr. Osbourne wants to work out those lungs to strengthen them." The nurse states.

"Ok."

"Aww do I have to do that today? Those exercises hurt and make me so tired!" Alexis whines.

"Well, Lexi, yes, it is necessary to get your lungs back in shape as soon as we can. This is all a part of your healing journey. Strengthening your lungs will help get you back to swimming. You need strong lungs to get your scuba certification in a few years." I say to my saddened child.

"But mooooom, it isn't fair!!" Alexis continues to cry.

My mouth tightens into a thin line. "No, baby, it is not fair."

I kiss her forehead and I excuse myself to her bathroom and I turn the water on in her sink, pull my phone out of my pocket to call Lorenzo. When he answers the phone, I growl lowly into the phone. "How are you going to make Rae pay for what she has done to Alexis? My baby is in pain, and the bitch needs to suffer!"

"Hey Mercedes, why are you whispering?"

"I am in her bathroom, trying not to scream."

"Oh, ok. I was going to come over to talk with both of you tomorrow. We went before a judge about it, and she was denied bond. The defense is trying to use an insanity claim. Her mother attempted to certify her incompetent to stand trial, and I countered that we will have an unbiased psychiatrist examine her. According to the jailers, she has been on 24-hour watch and, in their opinion, not doing well mentally."

"Oh hell no! She will not get away with this!" I growl

again.

"No, she will not. Even if she is deemed incompetent, she will never live a free day again. I will make sure that she is permanently institutionalized for life for what she has done to Lexi. If she is ever deemed to be competent, she will be tried and convicted. I will need to talk with Lexi's doctors and get her prognosis and the extent of her damages, and whether any are expected to be lifetime injuries."

"Of course, I will sign off on permission for you to discuss her condition with her doctors. Just make sure Raimer pays for all of it. I want to sue her insurance company for all medical expenses. Gut that ho."

"Heh, you know that I will. Uh, how is my twin? Is he doing ok? You haven't killed him or left him outside to rot have you?"

"You will see him tomorrow and can be the judge. Bring Lozanda. We will have dinner, we'll make it a night. I'll make your favorite, my mom's lasagna."

"Ooooh. That sounds amazing! It's a date. We will bring the wine. See you tomorrow at 7."

"That is perfect. See you then. I gotta go. I have to get

your brother out of the dungeon, and take him for a walk to let him get some fresh air."

"I know that you are joking. I do want to thank you for taking him and the twins in. You are the best there ever was. My idiot twin learned that too late. I hope that you two can work it all out. I love you, sis, see you tomorrow."

"Love you, too, bro. See ya. Bye."

"Bye."

I splash my face with cold water. Blot with a towel. Walk back into Alexis' room where the respiratory therapist is showing her how to use the breathing apparatus. Alexis has tears in her eyes as she concentrates on keeping the ball afloat inside the apparatus. The therapist is counting slowly and when he calls time, she falls back onto her pillow exhausted. I wave at them, and I head back to my room.

In my room Alex is sitting in a wingback chair looking at his laptop.

"Hey, how is our sweet girl?"

"She is having respiratory therapy right now. She says it hurts, and it leaves her exhausted. I called Lorenzo and almost cursed him out. Fortunately, he is on his p's and q's already, and I did not need to threaten him further."

Closing his laptop and setting it to the side. "That is a good thing. My brother is an excellent litigator, I have no fear that in the end, we will get the justice we need. Raemier will pay for what she has done. Do not doubt that."

"Yeah, we shall see."

"We shall."

"I know what Lexi means about these therapies we have to undergo. I was in excellent shape before the attack. Having to rebuild muscles that have been mangled by trauma is something different. I feel like I am unraveling knots every time. I want Rae put down for what she has done to us!" Alex spits venomously.

"They don't allow me to seek the death penalty for attempted vehicular manslaughter. I am not the state attorney." Lorenzo says to his twin, the two men are sitting in the office catching up.

"Too bad, but it would be so simple for all of us if she could be treated as a rabid dog. Every time the twins see me or their sister, they are livid with her. Adrian and Andre refuse to go see her, they have been resolute in their punishment of her. Adrian told me that he wants me to marry Mercedes so that we can be a whole family."

"Shiiiiiit. So how is that coming? Y'all made up?"

"Bruh, no not yet. We have been having the craziest sex. It is as if she is fucking a sex doll. No kissing. No touching. Just connected below the waist. She won't even look at me. Afterwards, she just dismounts and goes to take a shower."

Lorenzo just looks at his brother with a stunned expression on his face. "Dude, you have to fix that situation because it can only get worse if you don't. Fix it fast. However, I cannot imagine Mercedes being so cold-blooded. God damn, man."

"Yeah. But how? I am in no condition to turn the tables." Alex gestures to his arm and ribs and the rest of his body."

"Yeah, you need to use your words."

"You don't think that I have already? She does not want to hear it. She said that my failure to end relationships has us where we are now. Shenay showed up at the hospital to see me."

"No shit? Why?"

"She read about what happened on your FB post and decided to drive up. Mercedes did not know that we were still in contact with her. She thinks that Shenay was waiting for me to come to her, after my divorce."

"Yeah, Mercedes does have a point. Lozanda would have had me neutered if any ex of mine showed up in any capacity at my bedside."

"Lucky you, you have only one significant ex and Ashira is happily married with 3 kids and a dog in Maryland."

"Yeah? You know more than me."

"Heh, yeah, she and her husband are clients of mine, too. He is a doctor."

"You are messier than a bitch!"

"Shenay, Ashira, and so many others were my founding clients and have been with me since I started. I owe them a great debt. This is why they are all very wealthy. I work hard for all of them. They keep me on board and bring me new business. So much business, I have never had to market the firm. The way that those ladies network, they should be on my payroll." Alex chuckles.

"Wowwwwwww. That lasagna was delicious! Mercedes, you will have to ask your madre if I can have the recipe! Watching my husband shove it down like he did! I don't think I have ever had a dinner with these Sterlings all eating so focused and silent. Even the boys weren't their usual chatty selves." Lolo says, sipping her wine.

"I will ask her. Thanks!"

"Oh babe, you don't cook." Lorenzo says.

"I don't cook, you are right. It is not as if I can't cook. I am an Afro-Cuban. There was no way I was raised not knowing how to cook and run a home."

"Oh, so you just became Americanized when you married me?" Lorenzo says, further digging his hole.

"Bruh, what are you doing? You are making it worse! I thought that you were the smart one!" Alex says.

Lozanda taps her scarlet nails on the wine glass. "If you think that it is cold in the kitchen, it can get even colder in the bedroom." She smiles and raises her glass to me, and I raise my glass in return, we both share a laugh. With that Lorenzo stands up, takes Lozanda by the hand and begins walking her to the front door to leave.

"Uh, no ma'am, there will be none of that!" Lorenzo says as he stomps away.

Lozanda laughed even harder, "What? What did I say?"

"You know exactly what!" Lorenzo barks back.

Alex looks at me, arching his eyebrow and asks, "Really, Mercey, you told her?"

"Apparently you told Lorenzo, too!" I say chuckling.

"Yeah, we need to talk about that."

"We already have. Do you want this or nothing at all? I have been celibate a lot longer than you ever have been. You wouldn't make it if I cut you off completely.

You would think that you'd be happy with this arrangement."

"Yeah, you'd think so, but neither of us are 20-somethings and we have experienced the real thing together and we cannot go back to senseless, meaningless sex. We are too old for these games. I see how it is affecting you, rather affecting us."

"Yep, but we can discuss this after we get past this Rae and Shenay shit and see where we end up on the other side of that shit-show."

"We can go upstairs and call Shenay right now. Rae, that will take a long time to resolve. You heard Lorenzo, the trial won't be for a while. There is nothing we can do to rush that."

"Let's go call Shenay and bury this chick's feelings right now."

"I agree to air out her feelings, but I have no intentions of dropping her as a client."

"Oh?"

"I just want you to be clear. And, I will do the talking."

"Of course, it's your mess to clean up. Let's see if she

will still want to keep you on, afterwards."

"Come on. Let's do this."

"Hello?" Shenay answers on the first ring.

"Hey, uh, Shenay. This is Alexander. I am here with Mercedes, and she thinks that you were disappointed that we were back together. She even thinks perhaps you were hoping you and I would get back together after my divorce from Raemier."

"No, Alex. Thank you Mercedes for your concerns, but no. I am not pathetic, wasting 20 years of my life waiting for Alex. I can see how you would think that after my reaction in the hospital. All I can say is that I had just driven over 6 hours straight to the hospital. I was worried about my old friend being near-death. That is all. I am engaged to be married, myself. We have only been doing business, Merc. Actually, not once have we discussed anything other than my portfolio. You know, profits, losses, and more profits."

"Well, I am glad to hear that you aren't, using your words, pathetic, Shenay. I know that this is 20 years late, I want to apologize for any hurt that I have caused you. Congratulations on your engagement." I say.

"Heh, yeah. Ok. Well, now that that is settled, I am gonna go. Oh, and Alex?"

"Yes, Shenay?"

"Take care of each other. I wish you all the best. Finally, don't fuck this up, again. And get your head back in the game of making me my money!"

"I sure am not planning to fuck up again! My plans are always to make my loyal clients money, I will be in touch. Bye."

"Bye."

After hanging up, Alex turns to me and says, "There, are you satisfied?"

"You must think that I am boo-boo the fool. You guys just put on the best and biggest performance I have ever witnessed! Did you text her and tell her to say all of that?"

"Geesh! What the entire fuck do you want from me? I did text her to let her know that we were calling. I did not tell her what to say. We did the closure, you said 'we' needed. Stop picking it apart. Yes, I strung her along 20+ years ago, but not this time around, not since we reconciled. Yes, I blind-sided Raemier asking for a divorce after she wanted a temporary separation. Yes! I did that! That is all."

"Let me see your texts." I hold my hand out.

"Here." He hands me his iPhone. I look at his texts with Shenay and Raemier, and it is as he says. His conversation with Raemier is the most alarming. He told her that he hoped she had gotten everything she wanted because he was filing for divorce the next morning. No need to come back because the locks and alarm codes have all been changed. Because of the prenuptial agreement, she was not entitled to anything else. There was some name-calling from both. Then she states, "You will pay." There it was; it was sent the day she carried out her threat. It sent chills up my spine. And that was all.

I feel Alexander stepping closer to me, he lifts my chin to meet his eyes. "See?"

Tears are in my eyes.

"Raemier's message hit me hard."

"Yes, me too. To realize, she meant that shit, too. She meant with my life! I gave the text records to Lorenzo to show the judge."

I shake my head trying to reset my thoughts.

"May I kiss you?" He asks softly, running his hand up and down my arm.

"Yes." I whisper.

"Will you touch me?"

I slip my hands under his shirt, my fingertips softly grazing his skin underneath. Goosebumps spring up immediately. I gasp at his body's immediate response to my touch. I let him kiss me. The kiss is soft.

"Help me get these clothes off."

I nod. I walk to the door first and lock it. I return to his side. I unbutton his shirt, and slide it from his shoulders, I let it fall to the floor, I slide his pants over his hips, and they fall to the floor as well. I lead him to the bed. I slip out of my maxi dress. I help him into the bed. Once he is laying down, I pick up the jar of coconut oil from the night table. I take my hand and scoop out a small mound of the paste and place it in my mouth, it begins melting instantly when in my mouth. I lower my head to Alejandro, taking him in my mouth. I allow the oil to run down his length and I chase the flow with my mouth swallowing his length slurping the runoff oil back into my mouth as I do. Then rising back to his tip, I repeat the process. Making up for the lost time. No, everything is not forgiven, but I was being punished while I was punishing Alex. I needed the intimacy I was withholding from us.

"Ah ah ah ah ah" he says. "Ok! It is too much!"

I swallow. "What? Does it hurt?"

"Kinda. My ribs! You are making me tense up my entire body. I can't take it! It feels too good. That. Was. Fire! Climb up."

"Are you sure?"

"We have already been doing that. I know that I can tolerate that. But I want you to climb up on my face, though. I have no issues eating."

"Oh!"

I get in the bed next to Alex, we kiss deeply, and linger in the kiss before the rodeo begins. I slowly make my way to kneeling beside his head. I swing my leg across him and straddle his face, grabbing the headboard above us. I lower myself hovering above Alex. I wait for him to minister to my needs, which is building from the anticipation. Then, he sucks and licks my clitoris and then his tongue dives into my core. The sensuality of it causes me to buck my hips. He licks my core and sucks my clit, licking and sucking, over and over repeat, repeat, repeat and repeat. Fast then slow, ministering to my body's needs. He then takes his hand and slides his finger lightly down my spine. The sensation sends me soaring. My orgasm rockets my core, spasms open causing the dam to burst. I swear that I am drowning Alex, there is no way I am not. Thunder is happening, raging within me. I cannot maintain the position above him. I just climb off his ministering tongue.

"I have to tap out." I curl up next to him and just try to catch my breath and try to stop shaking. I have never felt all the feelings at once as I am now.

"Are you ok?"

"No, I don't know. I think that you broke me."

He chuckles, "Come now. I have never known you to tap out so quickly."

"Yeah, I know. I just felt my knees give out. I was about to collapse on your face and suffocate you. I tapped out to save your life."

"Awww, how sweet. I was never in any danger of suffocating, but drowning maybe, baby, you got juices flowing down my body."

"You broke me. Feel me, I cannot stop shaking."

"Shaking in a good way, right?"

"I… I guess. It felt good. That silver tongue of yours."

"Finally good for something, huh? Come on, let's continue."

I slowly rise and straddle his hips, sliding down his shaft and the quivering contractions return almost immediately."

"Oh, shit. You are still cuming."

"Yes. I am." I rock back and forth, and I curl up on top of Alex, trying not to put too much weight on him. My body contracts around his organ. This is amazing! How can something so simple as a suck, lick and a tickle connect to the innermost spot and send me into the strongest and longest orgasm I have ever had? EVER!

Raemier is unhinged, pacing the short length of her cell, talking to herself. He thinks that he can keep my sons away from me? Oh, he doesn't know what I will do to him and his whore. His life won't be worth shit, when I get through with him. He better bring his ass here and let me see my kids! Repeating, "He will pay! He will pay! He will pay!"

"Coochie quakes aside, what are we doing here?" I ask as I lay next to Alex.

"As I have said from the very beginning, I want you. I want us. I have been waiting for you to decide what you want. I have not changed my mind." He says.

"Hmmmpppfff. Well, when we started things were simpler. We weren't dealing with a deranged ex-wife and gun-toting teens."

"No, no we weren't. Andre and Adrian were always a part of the deal. Now Raemier has taken herself out of the equation because of what she has done, we will not have to fight her for custody. Do you want to move forward with me?"

"I know that I was the one who asked the question, but

I cannot answer that for you now. Right now, we are a happy blended family. With you, me, and all of your kids under one roof. Are we stable enough to continue and not blow up these kids' lives with our shit? I know we are physically magic, but will that magic flow through our day-to-day life? We still have a trial to go through."

"Yes, I know that we can do this. We both have to be committed to us to make it. I know that I am, are you?"

Am I? That is the magic question, am I? I stay silent and reflective. I stare at the ceiling listening to our individual breaths and imagine what it would be like if I were to allow this life to continue. I live here with Alexander and our three, his five kids. The seven of us. That sounds crazy to my chaotic mind. "Yeah, I do not know. I think we need to have a talk with all the kids and get a feel for what everyone is feeling."

"Uh, well, we are the adults here, we make the decisions for the entire family, we have the final say."

"Uh, yeah, but if everyone is not on board, teens have a way of making things very difficult for everyone else. I'm just saying, we need to get a consensus from everyone. I want Adrian and Andre to know that they have a voice in what happens to them, and they aren't just subject to the whims and fancies of their father's libido."

"Did you just say, 'subject to the whims and fancies of their father's libido'?"

"Yes [chuckling], I did! I have no idea how I can be so dramatic at times. I should be a novelist."

"Nah, there is no money in writing. Besides, what would you even write about?"

I look side-eyed at Alexander. "Number one, your exploits and all the tail chasing you have done for 31 of your 41 years would be enough for at least 3 to 5, New York Times best-sellers!"

"Hmmppf. No thanks. I am straight on that. Making me a villainous anti-hero is not my thing."

"You think too highly of yourself. I think I will just write it all down so I can process what is us."

"Not really because that was who I was back then, not who I am now. I do not want to keep being punished for that guy's deeds."

"True."

Months later, the day of Raemier's civil trial approaches. Lorenzo drops by the house to discuss what to expect.

A letter was delivered to Alexander at his office.

It is from Raemier. Her scrolling handwriting says:

"Alexander,

I am writing to you, against the advice of my counsel and my mother's wishes. The divorce happened so quickly. I was never given a chance to have my say.

When we began, long ago, I believed you when you told me you hated her. I believed you when you spoke with contempt about her. I believed you when you told me you loved me. I did not know they were all lies until you left me to go back to her (after you called me a "fat, sloppy, piece of shit"). I had no idea that you did not know how to love anyone because I was raised in love. I had no idea someone I would choose to love would not be raised the same way. (Naive of me, yes.) At 18, I was so busy falling in love with your potential, and how you made my body feel that even now, at 40, I do not regret you. I had no idea the love I wanted you to give me and, as their father, our (my) sons was alien to you. Because of your trauma, you did not know what it was. Now, I have had to learn how to forgive myself for ignoring every sign that you weren't what I wanted nor needed; and, to forgive you. The love I poured into you was not what you wanted nor needed at the time. I want you to heal. But, only you can do the work for it. Now that I am gone, you have to forgive the ghosts of the past that consume you.

I pray for your peace and that Jesus will give you the wisdom you need for your journey. I am sorry for what happened. I hope that Alexis is doing well. Give my love to Adrian and Andre. I do want to see my babies. Please do not continue to keep them from me. Also, Happy belated birthday.

Respectfully,

Baby mama #2

RS"

"What does she mean when she says, 'now that she's gone'?" Lorenzo asks.

"I have no idea. Maybe she should be on continued suicide watch? She is crazy. Nothing she says makes sense. She admits to hurting Alexis, maybe, we can use this letter to help convict her. I have no idea what she's talking about. We had a loving home growing up."

Alexander says.

"Remember this is only a civil trial. There won't be any convictions determined here; but yes, we can use the letter, and make sure that the State prosecutor has a copy of it." Lorenzo says.

"Right. I keep forgetting. We first must prove her culpability in what she did. Then, she goes to trial to face the criminal charges. Am I obligated to take the twins to see her?" Alex asks.

"No, you are not. They are old enough to say whether they want to see her. From what I understand, from our conversations, they do not want to see her."

"No, they do not. I also have not been encouraging them to see her. Neither has her mother. We steer clear of that topic."

"Then that is settled. Did you really tell her those things about Mercedes, that you 'hated' her?"

"No, yes, maybe at the beginning. I may have led her to believe that. I never hated Mercedes; but, when I was juggling two or three relationships, I would say anything to Rae to ease her ego."

"I never understood how or why you would ever feel

the need to be with anyone else other than your wife."

"Yeah, I don't recommend it to anyone. I had been dealing with Rae since high school, I never ended anything back then. I just strung girls along and did whatever I wanted with whomever I felt like being with."

"You have always been the whore."

"Yep, yep, yep, that was me."

"Being your twin has been a constant dodging of angry women. That is why I am glad that I went to Howard, and you went to FAMU. The first year separated from you was harder than I thought it would be. Then I met Ashira, and it got easier."

"Awww yes, regular pussy seems to have that effect."

"Wait a minute, you won't be reducing my first love to just her body parts."

"My bad, bruh, my bad. You are right, ain't no way I cannot understand that. I would whoop your ass, if you talked that way about my Mercedes."

"No doubt. How are you two doing these days? Are we any closer to walking back down the aisle?"

"Not, yet. We are talking to the kids about it this weekend."

"So, what are you going to do about your house? Obviously, you won't need it."

"Yeah, I do not know. I want to keep it to pass down to the kids, especially the twins. It was their home. They can decide what they want to do with it in the future. I really do not want it to just sit there unoccupied. I have no interest in renting it out because tenant wrangling isn't my thing."

"Yeah, we can run it by Lolo and see what she thinks. Real Estate is her wheelhouse."

"Yes. Let's wait on that for now since we still do not know if we are headed in that direction yet. I know that I am, but I still am not certain about Mercedes."

"Make it happen. Call your jeweler up and have a ring ready for this weekend when you talk to the kids. Do it up, bro. Like only you can do."

"You know what? You are right! I will do it."

"Well, alright."

All week Alexander has been acting very secretively,

spending a lot of time in Alexis' room having meetings with the kids. All are engaged with some big secret. Alexis has been giddy every time I go in to see her. She smiles like the Cheshire Cat when I walk into her suite. She just lays in her hospital bed, and, when I ask her what's going on, she just smiles even wider. Last night she said,

"In due time, all will be revealed, mama."

Saturday morning, after a light breakfast, I return to my suite to see Alex in my closet picking out a blush pink summer dress I have not worn yet. He holds it up and says,

"Wear this today."

"Why? What's the plan for today?"

"We are just spending time with the kids. We will have to do it in Alexis' room but I set up a movie screen and the projector so we can watch a special movie."

"Oh, ok. I was planning on meeting Mommy, Mother, Maria, and IsaMara for brunch, but I suppose we can make arrangements for another day."

"If you do not mind, I would greatly appreciate your indulging us. So, you'll wear this then?"

Taking the dress from his hand, "Yes. I will wear it." I say.

"Then I look forward to seeing it on the floor later tonight." He says winking and kisses me softly as he walks by.

One hour later, I received a text from Alex to meet in Alexis' room in 10 minutes.

Walking up the staircase I meet Adrian, he hands me a small bouquet of pink roses, and he smiles and gestures for me to continue. Then, I see Andre is waiting for me a few steps ahead. He is also holding a bouquet of white roses for me. On the landing stands Aren smiling at me. He hands me a third bouquet of roses; and, this one is white with pink on the tips of the petals. Aren leads me into Alexis' room, where Avery is waiting for me standing in the center of the sitting room smiling holding up his camera.

"Hey mom. We wanted you to know that we are all in agreement with putting our family back together. We want it. We need it."

With that, Alexander wheels Alexis into the room's center.

"Yes mama!" Says Alexis

"Yes, Mimi!" Says Adrian and Andre as they walk into the room.

Alex walks up to me, then kneels slowly in front of me. I gasp, as tears begin to roll down my face. I look at Alexander kneeling before me. Aren, hands me a tissue and takes the bouquets from my hands.

"It has always been you, Mercedes. I knew it when we were kids playing school, in grade school in our grandmother's classrooms. It was you when I saw you dancing with bum assed Clarence at the cotillion, for your debut. It has always been you. My heart is yours. When I thought that I would not ever see you again, you were my last thought before losing consciousness. When I wake up every morning, it is you whom I want to see first. These kids are blessed to have you as their mother, would you accept me so I can have you as my wife, again?"

Looking at each loving face staring at me. I smile and say, "Yes!"

Everyone cheers. Alex slides the even larger ring on my finger and rises to kiss me long and deeply.

"Aww mom, dad! Please!" Avery complains as he takes pictures with his new camera.

"Hush Avery! I think it's beautiful!" Alexis chastises her brother.

Aren, Adrian, and Andre all step in to hug us, and pose for Avery.

"Let's watch the video dad had us prepare for you!" Avery says.

We sit down on the blankets that have been placed on the floor. Avery starts the video. It begins with me at 7 years old standing between Alexander and Lorenzo. I am smiling and Alex is smiling coyly at the camera, his arm is around my shoulders and his hand appears to be pushing Lorenzo away.

"See, even then at 9, I knew."

I laugh, "Where did you find this picture?"

"Nana gave it to me when we got married the first time."

Then there are more pictures of us at family cookouts, high school games where Alexander is playing basketball with me cheering in the background.

"How on earth were you able to find all of these pictures?" I ask.

Then music begins to play, and the recording of our wedding begins. There is footage of people walking into the church. Briefly, you see a woman walking past the camera. The woman is wearing sunglasses, and she ducks her head when she sees someone she recognizes.

"That was mama." Adrian whispers.

"Yeah, it was." Andre says.

"I had no idea she came to our wedding." Alex says quietly under his breath. He looks at me, shaking his head remorsefully.

"Yeah. Me either. Apparently, no one did. She did not disrupt it." I say.

"Wait. I remember Janeese saying she had someone taken out during the ceremony. I wonder if it was her?"

After a few more minutes watching the ceremony, we see Janeese whispering to an usher and pointing at someone. The usher goes to a nearby pew and gestures to a woman, not Raemier, and walks her out of frame. The videographer zooms in tighter to focus on the actual ceremony taking place. There are two very young versions of myself and Alexander staring into each other's eyes repeating the vows Pastor Steve is reciting.

"So, who was that Janeese had removed?" I ask, "She walked by too quickly, I did not recognize her."

Clearing his throat, Alex whispers, "That was Ms. Thompson."

Scandalized, I gasp and look at him incredulously, "No! You didn't!" She was the basketball coach for our University.

Looking embarrassed he sighs. "Maybe I should have watched our wedding before and done some editing before giving it to Avery to put in my proposal video."

I push him lightly. "Oh no! You can't blame Avery!" I begin to laugh and think back to that day. I was so in love. I paid no attention to what was happening right in front of my face. Janeese was on alert. She knew her brother better than I did. She was looking out, but she missed Raemier. I wonder why she came? What was her plan? Was she so gluttonous for punishment that she would commit to watching her lover marry someone else? If it were me. I would not do it. This explains so much, how obsessed she has been all of these years!

Then, the video changes to our wedding reception and party. There was my father and daughter dance, my dad looking so handsome in his tuxedo tails, our first dance, the speeches from our siblings and parents, the cake cutting, everyone doing the electric slide, it was a grand time. I remember it all so well. There were pictures of us leaving for our honeymoon to Fiji with me glowing in every single photo; starry eyed glances at Alex in every frame.

Alex whispers, "I have had dinner delivered, let's go downstairs to eat." He stands and offers his hand to me. I take it and stand. I look at the kids and Avery says, "We are having pizza up here. I will have the nurse help me get Alexis back in her bed after we eat."

"Ok. Thank you, sweetie! Thank you all for this, it was magical! You all have made this a very special day for me!"

"Us too, Mimi!" Adrian says.

On the lanai, Alex had arranged a small table with white linen service to be set up. This included a gold candelabra with three tapered candles sitting ablaze in the center and there is a gloved server standing nearby with two covered dishes waiting to be served. Alex pulls out my chair and helps me to be seated. He walks around the table and seats himself across from me.

The server sets a dish in front of each of us, and with flair he removes each cover to reveal filet mignon, scalloped potatoes, greens, and bacon wrapped scallops.

"This looks delicious, Alexander."

"Yes, so, tell me, is there any way I will be able to get out of having to discuss Raemier or Ms. Thompson crashing our wedding 15 years ago?"

I laugh, "No sir, and if I am guessing correctly, you had sex with Ms. Thompson, right?"

"Yes."

"And you aren't on a first name basis with her yet?" I laugh again. I must ask Janeese what she was doing to get tossed out."

"None of that matters, now." He says.

"You are right, it doesn't matter since we are different people now. We aren't those kids anymore. I love my new ring with the flawless Emerald cut and a nice size.

It is evident that Raemier has always been obsessed with you."

"Yes, when I broke up with her, she never accepted it and would keep insisting that our relationship was not over. She sent me a letter to my office today. It sounds like she is still in that same headspace. It is disturbing, to say the least."

"What did she say in this letter?"

"Eh, I gave it to Lorenzo so he could use it in court. It shows she knew she injured Alexis in her attack."

"If it shows she isn't dealing in reality, it may even help her claim for insanity."

"Don't worry about it. It will be ok. My eyes are open and I am aware now of what we are dealing with. Seeing her in our wedding video opened my eyes to how deeply disturbed she really is."

"Seeing her there shocked me, too. What was her purpose for being there?"

"I have no idea. She never mentioned going."

"Never?"

"No, never.

"Hey, dad, can we talk?" Adrian asks a few days later, walking into the home office where Alexander has been working temporarily.

"Sure, come on in, son."

Adrian smiles, looks behind him, and walks in.

"What's on your mind?"

"I was just thinking about the other day, when you proposed to Mimi. You said that it was always her, but you still were with my mom even though you said you knew Mimi was the one you wanted as a little kid. How?"

Alex turns away from the monitor and looks at his son solemnly. "Yes, I was an ass to your mother and to Mimi back then. I was selfish and I wanted them both. Learn from my mistakes. When you meet the young lady that takes your breath with her when she leaves your presence, stay true to her and protect her from anything that would hurt her, even if it means you have to protect her from yourself."

"Do you regret having us?"

"No!"

"But having us hurt Mimi, right?"

"I may regret what I did to have you boys, but I never regretted you. Please understand that."

"Yeah, I guess." Adrian shrugs his shoulders and rises to leave the room.

"Wait, son, do you understand what I am saying to you? There is no universe where I exist without you and Andre. I wouldn't be complete without either of you."

Adrian runs around the desk and hugs his father fiercely. He sobs. Andre runs into the office and hugs his father and brother.

"I was listening at the door." Andre croaks.

"You did not have to son. You should have come in with Adrian. Don't be embarrassed to talk to me. My door is always open to you both. Never doubt that. When have I ever denied you access to me?"

"You never have." Adrian starts, "but..."

"But mom used to tell us to not bother you because if we did, you would leave us for your real family."

Sobbing even harder. Alexander tightens his arm

around the boys shakes his head. "No! No! No! That is not true! Does this have anything to do with you having a gun that day at the park?"

"Yes! I was so angry, I took mom's gun out of the box she had in the storage room at Aunt Lucinda's house, she didn't know I had it. Only Adrian knew about it."

"It was your mother's gun? How long had she had a gun? I know that I had guns in my safe, but I did not know she had a 9mm."

"Yes, she had one. I saw her pack it when we left. I don't know how long she had it, but she kept it under the mattress in your bedroom. She packed it before the movers came to take the bed."

"She kept it under the mattress in the bedroom?" Alexander repeats. Alex is just putting together how precarious his life had been when living with Raemier. She could have killed him at any time!

After talking to the twins, a shell-shocked Alexander makes his way upstairs to talk to me about what he has found out about what happened. After filling me in, I hug Alex and I leave him to find the twins.

I knock on their door.

"Yes?"

"It's Mimi."

"Come in."

Walking into their shared room.

"Hey." Looking at their tear-stained faces, I am at a loss for words. The thought that they never felt they belonged to Alex and the constant fear that he would leave them behind is unimaginable. The idea that a mother would have been the author of lies that would hurt her own children is beyond sick and just plain cruel. I look at these two precious boys and my heart goes out to them. I just stand there, open my arms to them, and beckon them to my open arms. Adrian looks at Andre who nods, and they both run to my embrace. Nearly knocking me over. They hug me so tightly I need to gasp for air. They are crying again, heaving sobs, and sniffing loudly.

Between gasping sobs, I finally say, "I am so sorry you doubted you would be wanted! Adrian, Andre you both have a home here for as long as you want it! I am your Mimi, never forget that I can never take the place of your mother. But just because you did not grow beneath my heart, you are in my heart. I am sorry if

I ever caused you pain or to doubt how I really feel about you."

"No ma'am. Whenever you did something with, um, your kids you took us with you. You took us to the Magic Kingdom for the first time, and when The World of Harry Potter opened at Universal Studios you took us!" Andre said.

"But more than just taking us to every theme park we have ever gone to, you are always kind to us. You have been more of a mother to us than our own mother has ever been. She has always been fixated on sadness and dad. I did not realize how crazy she was until I saw her in your wedding pictures. Let's be real, that ain't a sign of good mental health!" Adrian says.

"No, it isn't. Mimi?"

"Yes, Andre?"

"Um, when you re-marry our dad will you be our mom, too?"

"Well, sweetheart, I would love to be your mom. I have no desire to hurt your mother in that way. As a mother, I know how painful it would be to have my children call someone else mother. Especially, the woman she blames for everything that has gone wrong in her life." I replied.

"If she ever treated us as if we were her children, it would be different. We see how a mother is supposed to treat her children when we see you. The way you treat us is how a mother should treat her kids. We never had that before, we were just her way of keeping dad." Andre says soberly.

Alexander walks into the room joining the three of us. "That is an astonishing observation from such a young man. Mercey, the twins asked if you would be willing to adopt them?"

Adrian and Andre both look up at me, with expectant eyes. Pleading with me.

"Do you think that this is wise? Don't you think it would be what would break Raemier further?"

"But, Mimi, she has no need to be our mom, she's going to jail for what she's done to dad and Alexis!"

"I don't think you realize that she would have to give up her parental rights as your mother. It isn't so simple!" I say.

I look at Alex for help. "Boys, give her some time to

think about it. Your Mimi is kind to worry about your mother's feelings. Because she possesses empathy, she feels the pain it would cause a normal mother to face the reality that she has failed at being a mother to her children. Even with all that has been revealed Mercedes still has not spoken ill of your mother."

I look at the twins and they both nod their heads in understanding. I hug them tightly again. "You guys gave me a lot to think about. I will let you know. The trial starts in three weeks, will you be going with us? This will be the first time you will see her since her arrest."

They look at each other and nod. "Yes, we'll go."

"Ok, then, I am going up to take a bath, you men have exhausted me!"

They laugh and each boy kisses me on the cheek.

"Thank you, Mimi!" They say in unison.

"That twin-connection, I have to get used to it!"

"Yes, ma'am! "they say together and laugh at each other.

I laugh, too. I walk past Alexander, he stops me briefly

and whispers "I will be up shortly to join you."

I look back at the twins, "Good night. Do not stay up too late. Your dad is taking you off your punishment tonight, right, Alexander? Give them the packages that were delivered earlier."

"Oh yes. Follow me to the office Adrian and Andre."

In the office are two iPhones and MacBooks for the twins. They exclaimed with delight. Taking their boxes, they run back to their room to set up their new devices.

"Thanks dad!"

"You are welcome. Just stay out of trouble! No porn sites, please!"

"Yes sir!"

He heads to the stairs shaking his head, looking up he begins the climb. She is waiting for him, he feels the pull and with each step closer his heart races. He will soon be with her. Alex gets to the top of the stairs and turns left to walk to the bedroom and when he walks into the room, sees Mercedes on the floor in a heap and rushes to her side.

"Mercedes!!!"

Kneeling next to her, he reaches for her, turning her onto her back. She opens her eyes, eyelids fluttering. "What happened?" She asks.

"I have no idea! I just walked in and found you here on the floor!"

"I don't know. I just felt lightheaded when I came into the room."

"I am going to ask one of Alexis' nurses to come and check you out."

"Yes, ok."

Moments later, Alex returned with nurse Holly who wheels in her tool cart to check my blood pressure temperature, heart, and oxygen rate.

"Everything reads normal. Blood pressure is a little on the low side, 91/70, your temp is 98.7 normal, heart rate is 77 bpm also within a normal range. Oxygen is at 99%. How do you feel now, Mrs. Sterling? I understand that you have had some excitement in the past few days, congratulations are in order?!"

"Yes, I feel fine. Yes, we are engaged to be re-married."

Can you take my blood pressure again?"

"Sure! Of course!" Holly says. Placing the cuff back on my arm. She starts the monitor to measure my blood pressure. It beeps after several minutes "110/80 that is better! Pulse is at 80 bpm now."

"Ok thank you, nurse Holly." Alexander says as he walks her to the door.

When he returns, he sits down carefully next to me on the bed.

"When was your last cycle?"

I pick up my phone to look at the app I use to track my cycle. My hand begins to shake as I realize that I am over two weeks late. I am never late. I look at Alexander and I shake my head. "I am over two weeks late." I say shakily. Alex takes my hands and kisses me softly and says.

"Ok."

"Ok? No, not ok!"

"It is ok. We have been fucking like 20-year-olds, we sometimes use condoms but sometimes we do not." He lifts my chin to meet his eyes. "It is ok."

"Can you marry me without me being pregnant before we say 'I do'?"

"Apparently not!" He laughs and kisses me again.

Monday morning, I go to see my OB/GYN. Alexander comes with me.

The nurse has me pee in a cup and draws blood to check both for pregnancy hormones. We were left in a sterile examination room waiting for Dr. Pademi. Alex sits calmly next to me, I sigh.

"Remember almost 12 years ago we were here for the exact same thing?" He says.

"Oh! I remember! I was just as shocked as I am now!"

"Come on, you can't really be shocked. We haven't been exactly careful, have we? It was bound to happen! I can actually say that I am happy about this, if we are pregnant, we can do it right this time."

Dr. Pademi taps on the door and enters the room. She is a petite middle-aged, very jovial mannered, South Asian woman.

"Well, look who's here! It hasn't been a year yet, has it? You aren't due for an exam yet, Mercedes? Oh, you have the ex-husband here, too? It has been a while hasn't it, uh, Alexander is it?"

"It is, you have an excellent memory Dr. Pademi. It has been a while. You delivered my three babies in the last 16 years, and we are here to see if there is a fourth on the way."

She looks at me over her glasses. "Ah-ha, I see!" She sits down at the computer terminal and logs in. She reads Mercedes Quintero-Sterling, you are 39 years old, three healthy vaginal delivery pregnancies the last was 11, almost 12 years ago, so now you think that you could be with child again? That is possible. Looking at the urine test we just did, it's positive."

I gasp. Alex takes my hand and gently squeezes it.

She continues talking, "so, that reaction means you aren't too happy with this news?"

"No, well, my concern is that I had postpartum depression with the last one and we were divorced soon after for unrelated reasons."

"Oh, but you are in better circumstances now, aren't you?" She asks.

"Yes, we are, but having another child is unexpected!" I say.

"Oh? So, you haven't been doing the things you need to do to get pregnant?"

Laughing, Alex says, "Oh, we have most definitely been doing ALL the right things to get pregnant!"

She begins to laugh as well. I shake my head at them both.

She clears her throat and says soberly, "do you want to wait for the hemoglobin test results to come in before we get ahead of ourselves? If you are only a little late for your menses, we want to be sure that it is not a false-positive. Looking at the chart, if you are indeed pregnant, you would be around a month, 4 weeks, or so along. It is still pretty early. We can do an ultrasound and see if there is anything in-utero."

"How long will the blood test take?" I ask.

"I should have it within the hour. It pays to have our own in-house lab."

Dr. Pademi returns to the exam room, wheeling in an ultrasound device. "Well, it is another positive. I brought in the ultrasound in case you wanted to try and see what is happening?"

I look at Alex, he smiles and nods. "Yes, ok." I lay back on the exam bed and lift the paper gown up to expose my belly. She applies a gel to a long wand. Then slides what looks like a condom over the wand.

"I will need to do this vaginally. The embryo would be too small to see otherwise. Please put your feet in the stirrups and slide your hips all the way down to the edge of the exam bed." She says.

She inserts the wand and begins to move the wand in back-and-forth motions looking for my uterus on the monitor.

"We may be too early to see a fetus. What I am actually looking for is the uterine sac where the baby would be. Ahhh here it is!"

She turns the screen so that we can see. There in black and white is a black void with two peanut-sized nuggets there.

"Twins?!?" Alex stands up quickly.

"Wait. No!" I gasp.

"Yes, it appears to be so." Dr. Pademi says with a smile.

I am in shock as I dress, and on the ride home, I remain silent. Alexander is on cloud 9, chatting away. Talking about having a huge wedding before the babies arrive.

"Babies, with a fucking "S"!" I say finally able to speak.

"Yes, that's right." He replies.

"How the fuck are you so calm about this?" I ask

"I choose to be. What can we do? It has happened now we just have to prepare for them. Simple, right?" He surmises.

"It is easy for you to say, your part is over. Now I have the responsibility of making sure they get here without issues and that I come through this in one piece. You heard her say that I would be considered high risk because I am almost 40." I look at Alex and he sighs.

"I see it this way, it is a choice you must make. Either you can be happy about it and move inside that happiness or be miserable and move accordingly to negative energy. I am hoping that you will join me on the happy side, Mercey, we can do this!"

Looking down at the printed ultrasound picture of the two peanuts growing inside of me. I look back at Alex, I rub his smoothly shaven head, he shivers slightly, and I smile at his response to my touch. "They look like you." I say.

He laughs and kisses my knuckles. "So, when do you want to get married?"

"Now that the timeline has been established and I do not want to be fat and wobbly walking down the aisle. How does 2 months sound? I do not want another big wedding since we did that already."

Kissing my hand again. "Aww, man! I wanted to go bigger this time around. Have a huge party, since this will be our final walk down the aisle. This is it for us, baby!"

"What do you want to do?" I ask.

"I think you know what I am going to say. And I am your Disney BAE, after all. Remember when we got married the first time, you wanted to do it in front of Cinderella's Castle at Magic Kingdom? But our moms vetoed that, insisting we get married in the church."

My eyes light up. "Yes! Yes! Yes!" I squeal.

"That's right, baby! It's time to party!"

It is quiet when we walk into the house, I walk straight

into the kitchen, look at the fridge and I slap the ultrasound photo on the front and snap two magnets on it to hold it up. I open the door, pick two peaches and bite into one.

I look back at Alexander and smile, "I am choosing happiness. Let's see how long it takes these kids to notice this." I point at the picture, then tossing Alex the other peach, he catches it and takes a bite. Juice pools at the corners of his mouth, and I walk over to kiss him clean.

Fine'

BROKEN

The Author

Carmen N Arenas

Carmen, a native Floridian, is a single mother of two, and lives in Florida peacefully with her feline purrbabies.

www.ingramcontent.com/pod-product-compliance
Lightning Source LLC
Chambersburg PA
CBHW060345310726
48976CB00003B/729